A
Harlequin
Romance

KYLE'S KINGDOM

by

MARY WIBBERLEY

HARLEQUIN BOOKS

TORONTO
WINNIPEG

Original hard cover editon published in 1974
by Mills & Boon Limited.

© Mary Wibberley 1974

SBN 373-01836-3

Harlequin edition published December, 1974

Printed in Canada

1836

CHAPTER ONE

THREE months can be a long time. Isla Duncan had seen the calendar, and the thought came into her mind, and she smiled to herself. The last three months hadn't been, they had flown past in a blur of contentment because for the first time since childhood she had escaped the stifling domination of her father. She paused in her task for a moment to think about *that*. She had never imagined what it would be like to be free.

Voices came from the lounge next door, childish voices, a woman's softer lower response, the language they used Portuguese, a language she was finding to her astonishment that she now spoke reasonably well. She even thought in Portuguese most of the time, and that surely was the test. And in two hours Kyle would be calling for her to take her out. Kyle! The thought of him was a warm glow inside her. She had known him only ten days, but it could have been for ever, the effect he had on her. . . .

"Isla? You are very quiet!" The soft voice interrupted her thoughts, and she turned to see Maria Oliveira, her employer and friend, standing in the doorway to the kitchen.

"I was thinking." A quick glance at the clock on the wall. "Heavens, I'd better finish getting the boys' meal ready or they'll be starving."

Maria laughed. At thirty she was ten years older than Isla, a small dark attractive woman, mother of three lively boys, and a good friend and confidante to have. "You know, I don't ask you to be cook as well," she protested, her eyes sparkling with humour. "I can finish that. You go and get ready for your Kyle."

"There's plenty of time, he won't be here until nine."

"Where are you going tonight?" Maria's question, Isla knew, was not only idle curiosity, she had a genuine concern for Isla's welfare.

"I don't know," she admitted. "He says it's a surprise. So I'll just have to wait and see. But we won't be in late, you know that."

Maria gave a graceful shrug. "Ah, no, it is not that. It is just —" she paused, "you do not really know him very well, I mean —"

"Do you *like* him?" Isla asked softly.

Maria's blue eyes widened. "Yes, he is a fine-looking man, and his manners, for an Englishman, are quite exceptional — but you were not *introduced* —" She stopped at Isla's peal of laughter.

"Oh, Maria! I've told you, things are different in England, honestly — at least —" her blue eyes clouded slightly, "they are for *most* people. I've never known what it was like to meet anyone casually before. My father — and his money — saw to *that*."

The older woman nodded. "I know, I know, my dear. It must have been very difficult for you. You still write — to let him know you are safe?"

"Yes," Isla nodded. "I owe him that much at least. But he'll never find me, I've made sure of that too. The letters are posted from all over the place. He may know I'm here in Brazil, but it's big enough for him not to be

6

able to pinpoint the location."

"Ah yes, but if I didn't have a husband who travelled all over the country, and sent them off for you, what would you have done then?"

Isla smiled, shaking her head slightly. "I'd have found some way of letting my father know. I can't – I can't –" she faltered for a moment, then recovered, "I can't just forget him like that. But if you knew what it was like, being a prisoner –"

"If I had not understood, I would not have asked you to come here, Isla, and it was the best thing too. You are so marvellous with the boys, already they love you –"

A small figure hurtled through the door and flung himself on Isla with the cry, in shaky English:

"Luis is after me, save me!"

Maria laughed. "You *see*! Out you go, Adriano, at once, Isla and I are talking. Go!"

The chubby fair-haired boy pulled a face, and dragged himself reluctantly out.

Isla adjusted the heat under two pans, stirring one, with a tasty-smelling mixture of meat and vegetables, as she did so. All the cooking lessons learned at expensive schools were coming in useful – she had never imagined they would; her father had planned her life so well that it seemed inevitable she would marry some wealthy young man, virtually chosen by him, and would continue to lead a life of boring, useless luxury – the life that had so stifled her, and frightened her at the idea of a future stretching away. . . .

"Ah well, as you have everything well under control, I will not interfere. Believe me, Isla, you will never know what your company has meant to me here, with Roberto so often away –"

"Please," Isla protested softly. "The thanks are due from *me*. You helped when I needed it most. I can never repay that." And her mind went back irresistibly to her arrival in Rio de Janeiro, three months previously, exhausted after the long flight, the phone call made, the immediate invitation from the Oliveiras', whom she had met only twice previously when both Roberto and Maria had been guests of one of her father's managers in London, and she and Maria had discovered that they were both on the same wavelength. She had contacted them solely to find out if they knew of somewhere to stay, for she had known instinctively that she could trust them both. As a result of that call, the immediate invitation, and then the tentative proposition; would she care to stay and help with three unruly boys? Only the boys weren't unruly. They were lively and mischievous, but basically well disciplined, and Isla, who had never had any experience with children, soon found herself coping efficiently. A new life, something quite beyond her dreams.

And then, ten days ago . . . Kyle had walked into her life. Kyle Quentin, who had retrieved an errant youngest boy while Isla was pouring out orange juice from a flask for the two older ones as they sat on Copacabana Beach, and the sun was tempered with a gentle breeze. . . . She didn't notice Maria walk quietly out of the kitchen, a little smile on her face. She was there on the beach again.

"Is this one of yours?" The voice was deep and amused, one wriggling red-faced boy held firmly under a big man's arm. Isla had looked up quickly, eyes widening in

8

dismay. She scrambled to her feet.

"I'm so sorry, I don't know how –" She looked round to see Luis and Adriano looking innocently at her. "– I only looked away for a moment –"

"He was going at a fair lick down the sands." And then Isla realized what should have been obvious right away. The man had spoken in *English*.

"How did you know –?" she began, and he grinned as he deposited Marcos on the soft crunchy white sand.

"You were English?" he finished it for her. "I saw you yesterday, heard you call them to come." She watched him as he spoke; standing there before her, a veritable giant of a man with short sun-bleached hair and amused-looking greeny-blue eyes. He had a strong face, he was well built, tough-looking, dressed very casually in jeans and blue denim jacket and leather thonged sandals. A sudden warmth rose in Isla. He was looking at her in a certain way. . . .

"Thank you anyway," she said quickly, to cover up this treacherously weak sensation that was inexplicably filling her. This had never happened before, this vibrant feeling of instant empathy with a *stranger*. She didn't want it to show. It mustn't.

"They're not yours?" He had a wide mouth, now quirked in a disbelieving grin as he looked at the boys, then at her.

She could laugh at that. It helped to relieve the tension.

"No. I'm minding them. They're a friend's."

"Lucky friend," he remarked dryly, and it might have had another meaning, but she wasn't sure.

"Yes, well, thank you again, Mr. –"

9

"Quentin. Kyle Quentin. And you are Isla."

Her eyes widened. "H-how did –"

"No magic. When you hear it shrieked in a childish treble, you tend to remember it. Yesterday, when I passed, one of them shouted at you."

"Oh." Then she remembered. "Luis had found a valuable stone – at least he thought so," she smiled at the memory. "It was a piece of green glass, worn smooth by the sea." As if on cue, Luis proudly produced the object from the pocket of his brief blue shorts and handed it to Kyle Quentin, who gave a low whistle as he handled it.

"I see what you mean. You never know, do you?" but he watched Isla again as he spoke, and for some reason she had to look away swiftly.

The memories were still vivid. Isla hurried away from the cooker and began to fetch the plates from the cupboard to the table. After their brief unofficial introduction, the man called Kyle had stayed and before Isla took the boys back to the flat, she found much to her delighted surprise that she had accepted an invitation to a meal that evening. Maria had been horrified at first, only slightly mollified by the knowledge that Kyle would at least be calling for Isla, and had announced: "And if I think he is a wolf, I will insist on chaperoning you this evening!"

It hadn't been necessary. Kyle could charm the birds from the trees if he chose, Isla thought wryly. In the first few minutes after entering the apartment he had been quietly polite, enquired diffidently if Maria and her husband would care to come out with them, thus sweeping any fragment of resistance away before it even arose. Maria was regretful. Alas, there were baby-sitter problems; and she had looked at Isla when Kyle wasn't looking, and had nodded, and winked in a way that meant only one thing. . . .

They had been out almost every evening since then. Kyle hadn't even attempted to kiss Isla on that first, most pleasant evening out, nor on the second – which, perversely, had annoyed her. She knew how to deal with importunate young men, but how did you deal with a man who appeared to like you a great deal, but found you quite resistible physically? It had been almost a relief when, at the end of the third evening out, while they were walking along a darkened passage leading to the rear entrance to the apartment, he had paused and then pulled Isla gently towards him. "Just a moment," he had said softly, in that dark exciting voice, "there's something I meant to do –" and then he had kissed her. She had been kissed before, but only ever by father-approved suitors, almost uniformly dull. This was so different as to be unbelievable. After the first startling, tingling moment, Isla had melted into his arms, responding, with an eagerness that almost shocked her, to the warmth of his exciting lips. . . .

And now, as she waited for the hour to pass until he arrived, Isla wondered if she was beginning to fall in love. She was ready at nine, putting the finishing touches to her make-up in her bedroom when the doorbell chimed. She smiled to herself. Kyle had never been a minute late. If he said nine, then nine it was, not before, or after. She heard Maria's voice faintly in greeting, the deeper tones in reply, then laughter, and then silence as the door to the lounge closed behind them. She pulled a face at her reflection, wishing vainly that her dark hair

11

were straighter, instead of with its rebellious curl that de-fied combs and brushes. Her face stared back at her, tanned to a warm gold by the Brazilian sun, a dusting of freckles on her nose, her mouth wide and soft, her eyes blue, darkly lashed, the whole effect one of warm dark beauty of which she was quite unselfconscious. She picked up her white handbag, adjusted the strap on one sandal – and crossed to the door.

"Hello, Isla." Kyle was standing by the window as she went in and he walked towards her to greet her. He was dressed in dark blue blazer, grey slacks, and a white shirt that set off his suntan to perfection. His eyes held hers warmly as he smiled and reached out to take her hand, watched approvingly by Maria. An unopened box of liqueur chocolates was on the table beside the older woman. So it was her turn this evening. Kyle never came empty-handed – sweets for the children, or flowers or chocolates for Maria.

"You will have coffee before you go, Kyle?" Maria enquired.

"No, thanks. I've booked a table for ten – and it's nearly an hour's journey." He looked at Isla. "Ready?"

"Yes. Where are we going?"

"Wait and see." He grinned at Maria and winked. "Do you think she'll like it?"

"I'm sure she will. Away you go, then. You have your key, Isla?"

"Yes, Maria."

"Goodnight, Maria. I won't bring Isla home too late."

His red Volkswagen was parked a distance away and her heels click-clacked on the pavement as they walked towards it. The black velvet sky, diamond-studded, was a perfect setting for a night out, and the air was still warm from the heat of the day. Kyle took Isla's hand as if it were the most natural thing to do and she curled her fingers round his, feeling the warmth and strength. . . . People brushed past them, intent on their own affairs.

"Happy?" he enquired softly.

"Yes. And you?"

"Of course." He laughed as if surprised. She always liked to hear his laugh, deep and full. "Why wouldn't I be happy when I'm with you?"

She shook her head slightly. She had never met anyone like him before, never seen him as anything else but charming and full of good humour. Yet even so, she sensed there would be another side to his character, a depth, a mystery, for sometimes, when she had looked at him, and he had not been aware of her glance, she had glimpsed something that puzzled her. Now was not the time to think of it, however, for there was an evening ahead of them, just the two of them, and they were clearly going somewhere special. . . .

"Ready? Comfortable?"

"Yes, thanks." She flung her bag on the back seat and checked that her seat belt was fastened. Kyle drove swiftly, but she had perfect confidence in him. The miles flashed past, Rio was left behind and they were still going, but now Kyle seemed to be slowing as he drove along. They turned up a wide side road, changing gear as they began to climb. Higher they went, and looking back, Isla could see distant ocean, dark and fathomless with a high bright moon casting its ghostly sheen over everything.

Lush fields stretched away on either side of them, and cars were fewer, and everything was quiet.

Kyle drew into the side of the road and switched off the engine. "Before we reach our destination," he said, "I've got something to ask you. How do you fancy a few days' holiday with me?"

She turned slowly to look at him, and something of what she was thinking must have shown in her face, for he shook his head slowly as if amused. "Oh no, Isla! Come on, say it."

She closed her eyes briefly. "Say what?"

"What's written so clearly over your face: 'So this is the proposition coming up.' Isn't that what you're thinking?"

"I don't know," she shook her head. "What am I expected to think?"

"Simply that I've asked you if you'd like to have a few days' holiday with me – and that's all. No strings attached. Or, to be perfectly blunt – I don't intend to try and seduce you, that's a promise."

She let out her breath in a long sigh. "Oh, Kyle, I'm sorry. It's just – I've never been asked – like that before."

"No? There's always a first time, isn't there? I thought you'd jump at the idea. Maria and her husband won't mind, will they?"

She shook her head. "No-o, I don't imagine so. You've impressed them as being terribly 'unwolfish' – and in any case, I'm a free agent now."

"Free agent now," he repeated the words in a question. "Heavens, what does that mean?" Isla had never told him anything of her past, and he had never asked. It was not something she even wanted to discuss – not even with him; not yet anyway. Soon – she might feel able to tell him.

She smiled. "A slip of the tongue. Forget it."

"Consider it forgotten. Well, what about it?"

"I'd love to," she answered promptly. "When?"

"Next weekend. Do you like flying?"

"It doesn't bother me. But where to?"

"You'll see. You trust me, don't you?"

"Yes," she answered simply.

"Well then." He shrugged and reached out to switch on the engine. "Bring your swimsuit."

She laughed. "I've got three. I'll take them all." She didn't see the odd look he gave her as the engine rumbled into life. She was too busy thinking pleasant thoughts. The look would have puzzled her. It was better for her peace of mind that she was quite unaware of it.

With Kyle, Isla decided, it was a case of no sooner said than done. It was Friday morning just after breakfast, and they were flying several thousand feet up, with Rio already over a hundred miles away. She shook her head, bemused, and looked around her. She had expected they would be going on a scheduled flight from Rio airport to their mysterious destination, which was why the effect of Kyle's words on reaching the airport had so stunned her.

"I've got my own plane," he had said, then, amused, seeing her face, "Oh, didn't I tell you?"

"No, you d-didn't," she answered faintly, and looked at him. What sort of man was it who could spring a thing like that on you at a moment's notice?

15

Something stirred inside her. Even the most blasé of her father's wealthy acquaintances would have managed to drop a fact like *that* into the conversation before now – but Kyle, sweet, *mysterious* Kyle with his casual clothes and old red Volkswagen, had apparently forgotten.

As they walked towards a far quieter corner of the huge airport complex, she wondered what exactly he was – *who* exactly he was. He had never spoken about work, or money, or his background, and Isla, only too aware of her own secrets, had not asked. There had been too many other things to talk about anyway that it hadn't seemed to matter. Now, the first pangs of doubt assailed her, and she slowed her footsteps imperceptibly so that Kyle, slightly ahead, carrying both their cases, asked: "What's up?"

She shook her head faintly. The day was brilliantly hot, faint perspiration beaded her face, and her yellow sundress clung to her slender figure.

"I don't know. It's just – this –" She pointed to the waiting plane, a small jet, silver-grey, gleaming in the sun's rays, waiting for them.

He laughed. "Want another look at my passport? I'm no white slaver –"

"It's not that," she had to smile, and caught up with him then. "But you never *said*."

"You never *asked*! Hey, you're not frightened, are you? You did say –"

"No." They were there now, and he reached up, a tall man who could do that easily, and reached down the foldaway steps for them to get in.

"No," she repeated the word firmly. "I'm sure you're

a good pilot. I'd trust you anyway," and she looked up and smiled at Kyle, and for a moment they stood there facing each other. She looked quite beautiful when she smiled; it was happy, and her eyes lit up with pleasure when she did so, and for a moment the man called Kyle looked at her with no answering smile on his own face, then he reached forward to take her arm.

"We'd better get aboard," he said, and it was odd, but his voice was almost harsh. And his eyes had a bleak, shuttered look.

Her eyes closed after a while. She knew their destination now: Trintero Island, over two thousand miles away from Rio, near the West Indies, and a place where Kyle had business. He had ventured no further information, and Isla had not asked. He would tell her what he wanted, anything else could wait. He was a different person once aboard the beautiful aircraft; whereas before he had managed to give the impression of a casual happy-go-lucky man, now there was a decisiveness, almost a hardness, about him. Lying there resting against the seat, she saw again his face as it had been just before boarding the plane. It had been puzzling, that bleak look, almost frightening, but she had said nothing, merely gone aboard, and then forgotten it in the wonder of looking round at the neatly appointed interior.

There were only eight seats, blue-upholstered, four at each side of the aisle, well spaced out, obviously custombuilt. Isla had turned to him, eyes wide.

She was used to wealth, it had been part of her life since birth, luxury, money unlimited, but he was not to know that, and what would he think if she showed no surprise? And it was beautiful anyway, so there need be no half truths. "I'm absolutely stunned," she admitted. "Is that the galley?"

"Yes. You can make us a cup of coffee when we're on our way," and this time he smiled. The bleak look had gone, and might never have been. It might even have been her imagination. But she knew, deep down, that it was not.

"Isla?" his voice roused her from her introspection, and she sat up.

"Yes?" She was already on her way to the cockpit as she answered. There was no sensation of movement, only the deep heavy thrum of the powerful motors beneath her as she made her way and waited inside the door.

He didn't look round. "May I have another coffee, please?"

"Of course, Kyle. Anything to eat?"

"No, not yet. You can. Are you hungry?"

She laughed. "No. Can I sit with you while you drink it?"

He turned slightly then, and looked up at her. "Of course."

She went out and left him. In the neat, spotlessly clean galley she measured instant coffee into two beakers and put water on to heat. Far, far below, a vast mat of dark green that could have been grass, but were millions of trees, waited still and silent and mysterious. She shivered, suddenly cold, then the sensation passed. She made the coffee and took it along, walking carefully in case of turbulence, but there was nothing, just the faint vibration of power, and a thin shell between them and space.

"There you are."

"Thanks." He lit a small cheroot, and the aromatic scent filled the cabin. She watched him sitting there, seemingly relaxed, his hands on the wheel, arms and hands powerful-looking, as was the rest of him. She thought to herself, very suddenly: "I don't *know* you at all!" And the thought was not a little disturbing. But she said nothing, because it was too late now to change her mind. And she didn't want to anyway. . . .

"You're very quiet," he commented.

"I was just thinking."

He looked sideways at her, smiled briefly, then back again to look ahead.

She watched his profile. Long straight nose, full mouth, very stubborn-looking chin, he was most attractive, and she wondered again at her own feelings for him. He had rarely kissed her, but when he did, it was something special, she knew that. Was it, she wondered, also special for him? But that was something she could hardly ask. His hair was bleached by the sun, short hair that might originally have been light brown, it was difficult to tell. He had a good healthy tan, and when he smiled, his teeth were very white in contrast.

"Don't you get tired?" she asked suddenly, fearful he would have seen her regard.

"No." He seemed almost amused for a moment, but it passed. "I need very little sleep – and I could fly this thing anyway in my sleep –"

"Don't try!" she warned him hastily.

He shook his head. "Don't worry – I'm only joking. I'm aboard as well, you know." He pressed a lever, then took his hand from the controls. "See – she's on George now."

"Oh, the automatic pilot," she nodded, a little smile quickly hidden at the merest suspicion that he had hoped to confuse her.

"Ah, I see you know all about it. Right, it's all yours." And he stood up.

"But –" alarm flared, "you can't –"

"Oh yes, I can. Be back in a minute." And he vanished into the body of the plane.

Isla sat rigid for a few seconds, then slipped into his vacant seat. It was a strange sensation, the feeling that she was in charge of a plane, even though she wasn't, and she was very careful not to touch anything. Very careful indeed.

"That's enough. Move over." Mock stern, his voice came from behind her, and she looked up. He was half leaning over her, his face very near, and just for a second he might have been going to kiss her. . . . But he didn't, and the moment passed. Isla stood up and went to the co-pilot's seat, and sat down. Her heartbeat was erratic and for a moment she experienced an almost dizzy sensation. There was something different about him, but she didn't know what it was.

She turned away to look down at the country beneath them, everything tiny and toylike, barely seeming to move. Several more hours to go, with a man she was beginning to wonder if she knew at all, and she didn't even know the first thing about this island they were going to stay at. Trintero Island; only the name, a dot on the map. What, she wondered, would it be like?

CHAPTER TWO

THE night was well advanced, Isla had slept, and now she was woken by Kyle's gentle touch on her arm.

"We're here, Isla. Are you awake?"

"Yes." She yawned and stretched, then shivered. The plane was cool, her dress seeming too thin now. "Is this Trintero?"

"Yes. We're cleared with Customs, there's a car waiting. All we have to do is lock up and go." He bent over and unfastened her seat belt.

"Oh," and she stood up. Lights burned, soft quiet lights, and blackness outside, and no sounds. They could have been anywhere in the world. She looked at him. "Where are we going?"

"A hotel – you'll see. You'll like it. Come."

She waited shivering on the tarmac for him to jump down beside her. He took her arm and they walked away from the now darkened plane that was neatly parked, like some large car, at the edge of an airfield. Her eyes were getting used to the dark, adjusting rapidly, and in the distance there were lights and buildings and faint music. Nearer, the throbbing of a car engine, its sidelights on, and she climbed in, followed by Kyle.

"Goodnight, Isla. Sleep well. I'm next door if you want anything." He pointed to a louvred door and went to it. "Look, it's bolted now," and he locked it as he said the words, clicking it to with a decisive 'snap'. "I'll leave my side unbolted, but you've no worries, this is a very good place."

"I'm sure," she smiled at him, looked at him as he walked towards the door to the corridor. She had only the vaguest impression of the entrance to the hotel, except that it had been well lit, clean and spacious and very modern. She looked longingly at the huge fourposter bed, all white, soft and welcoming. "Goodnight, Kyle."

Isla bolted the door after him, cleaned her teeth and undressed. Five minutes later she was fast asleep.

She woke to see sunlight bursting in through the closed shutters, slanting goldenly across the tiled floor, touching the bed with warm fingers, rousing her. Isla sat up and stretched. She was hungry. Would Kyle be awake?

She went over to listen at the adjoining door, then knocked softly. Her watch had stopped during the night, so that she didn't even know what time it was. "Kyle? Are you awake?"

There was no answer, and alarm, like a soft fluttering moth, touched her spine. She felt suddenly alone, then the brief moment passed and she shook her head at her own foolishness. She went and ran a bath in the compact bathroom which led off from her bedroom. Hot water gushed out, and there was an ornate bottle of brightly violet-coloured and highly scented salts of which she put in a generous handful.

Refreshed and cool, she dressed in blue skirt and shirt top and unbolted her door.

"Morning!" Kyle's voice greeted her. He was walking along the corridor, dressed in brief white swimming trunks, his short hair glinting with water. A blue towel was slung around hs shoulders like a scarf and he was barefoot. He grinned at Isla.

"Did you wonder where I'd gone?"

"I called you when I woke – thought you were still asleep, so I had a bath."

"I've been up an hour. The pool here is quite something. Ready to eat?"

"Mmm, yes. I'm starving!" He was extremely well built, although she had imagined he would be anyway. Muscular shoulders and arms, long tanned hairy legs, and very attractive. She realized she was staring and dragged her eyes away.

"Oh, my bag – I'll go and get it." She went back into the room, and heard his voice as he went along to his own door:

"I'll not be a moment, just get some clothes on."

The dining room was cool, with potted palms and flowers giving a certain privacy to their corner table. They were watched in uncurious fashion by the only other occupants, two couples who appeared to be eating a gargantuan breakfast. Kyle shuddered as he sat down. "Did you see *that*?" he whispered.

"I can only manage coffee and toast. How about you?"

"I don't know." Isla smiled. "I rather fancied these syrupy things."

He pulled a face. "Your wish is my command." He caught a white-jacketed waiter's eye. "I thought you girls always had to watch your weight – although," he added thoughtfully, "I must say you always do justice to the meals on our evenings out." He ordered breakfast and turned back to Isla. "What do you want to do today?"

"I thought you came here on business?"

He gave a careless dismissive shrug. "That'll only take an hour or so. Later will do. The morning's all yours – and the evening."

"Can we tour the island? Are there shops?"

"Both. Is that what you want? I'll hire a car and we'll do it at our own speed. And then tomorrow –" and he paused, and she wondered what he had been about to say, for an odd expression came on his face. "Then tomorrow we'll call at another island, then back home."

"You're the boss," she agreed, but a slight frown creased her forehead as she watched him. What was it? Something wasn't quite right, her instinct told her; there was a certain tautness about him, not so much in his face as in his whole demeanour, a closed reserve that she had occasionally noted before.

She soon put the thoughts to one side as the waiter brought in breakfast, and a bowl of fresh fruit for after it, and Kyle exerted himself to be the attentive host, and the puzzled moments might never have been.

The car was waiting for them outside when they had finished eating, a smart blue Chrysler. Kyle opened Isla's door for her, and a minute later they were setting off down a wide sunny street lined with palm trees and bright flowering shrubs. Camera-clicking tourists rubbed shoulders with natives, and opposite the hotel was a market place with gaily coloured stalls loaded with produce, fruit, clothes, ornaments. Traffic was light, the main part seeming to consist of carts pulled by donkeys. Isla looked round her fascinated, taking it all in as Kyle drove slowly along. The buildings were modern and clean, and when they reached a long street crammed with every imaginable kind of shop, she turned to him. "What a super place," she said.

He laughed. "Yes. I'm quite fond of it. There's a cruise liner in today, that's why we've seen so many tourists. They come and load up with souvenirs they could buy for half the price anywhere else, and go back happy." He looked briefly at her. "We leave the town behind in a moment, then you'll see some scenery. You brought your swimsuit?"

"In the back, with yours. We're going swimming?"

"Only if you want to. Do you?"

"Yes, of course. But where?"

"You'll see. I'll guarantee you'll not see another soul. Then we can eat."

"And I suppose you know a little place tucked away in the hills?"

"How did you guess?" He laughed. "Don't forget I've been here before several times."

And who were you with then? But she wondered that silently. She imagined that Kyle would rarely be alone. He possessed a vitality, despite the air of calm she was beginning to appreciate in him. Coming from a world of wealthy neurotic people, as most of her father's business acquaintances and friends were, he was a refreshing change. More, he had a devastating charm and ease of manner, an inbred courtesy that was extremely relaxing. That was it – she could relax with him as she had never – or only rarely – been able to do before with anybody else. She looked curiously at him as he guided the car skilfully

25

along the twisting road. The sea sparkled in the sunlight, throwing up gauzy slants of gold that could dazzle if you looked at it long enough. The sky was a bright pale blue, with no clouds anywhere, and only the faintest breeze stirred the leaves of the many palm trees.

"I could stay here for ever." She didn't know why she should say it, and he glanced briefly at her.

"Just like that?"

Isla smiled. "I don't know what made me say it," she admitted.

He was slowing the car, turning right to take a bumpy track downwards. "Hold tight," he told her, and she put her arm along the back of his seat and held it. "We're nearly there." A steep sudden turn; she felt the surface change, become softer, and then he stopped the car.

"This is it. Like it?"

She looked ahead to the white beach stretching out in front of them, stretching away for miles and miles, and not a soul to be seen, only two gulls pecking at a pile of seaweed, and the white foamy breakers swishing in to vanish and melt into salty sand. Isla took a long deep breath. "Wow!" she said.

"Right, get your suit on. In the car if you can manage it. If not, just outside." He reached over to the back seat and lifted his trunks from under the two hotel towels he had brought out. "I'll go along behind that rock to change. Just shout when you're ready. I promise I won't peep." His door slammed, she watched him go, unbuttoning his pink cotton shirt as he went taking long loping strides, not looking back.

Isla gave a small secret sigh and reached behind her for

the dazzling yellow suit, her favourite. Kyle had completely vanished. She began to undress.

"Ready." She waited by the car for him to reappear, and when he did so, from behind the huge rock, she walked towards him. He flung his clothes on the driver's seat and took her hand.

"Race you!" But it wasn't really a race, because he had her hand, and pulled her along with him. They ran along, the sand soft and dry underfoot, leaving blurry footprints in an erratic trail behind them, until the first of the white bubbly foam was touching their feet, and he stopped, and pulled her near to him. "Do I throw you in?" he mused, almost as if talking to himself.

"You wouldn't dare!" And she tried to pull her hand free. He began to laugh.

"Dare? Now that's a challenge if you like," and he swept her off her feet and into his arms. For a moment she was too surprised to struggle, so quick had he been, then she flung her arms round his neck in an instinctive gesture of self-protection.

"Kyle –" she warned, beginning to laugh. But he was already walking into the water, and the way he held her, somehow she felt as if she were a featherweight. It was a pleasant new sensation. He waded waist-deep, and she could almost smell the water, its salty warm tang, and she shivered deliciously. "All right," she said, "drop me if you must," and she was already planning her revenge.

He shook his head. "Did you really think I would?" She was gently lowered, to stand in the water beside him, and after the first quick breathless shock, she found it pleasantly warm. "We don't swim out too far," he said.

27

"Sharks don't come this far in usually, but we won't take chances."

"Sharks!" She looked quickly down as if one might have sidled up unnoticed. "Oh!"

"We're quite safe here. Come on, race you along." He leaned forward and struck out, and Isla, after a bare second's hesitation, followed him. She forgot all about sharks in the next half hour, which passed in a golden haze of sheer delight as they swam and dived in the clear greeny-blue water. Tired, she lay on her back and floated for a while, and such a feeling of contentment filled her that she thought she would burst. How wonderful everything was! How wonderful *he* was.

"Penny for them," and she opened her eyes to see Kyle laughing over her. He had swum silently up and surfaced beside her and was standing beside her.

"Mmm? I was just dreaming," she answered. She couldn't put any other thoughts into words. She wouldn't have wanted to; they were too intensely personal. She looked at him. Sea water beaded his wet hair and face, and his tan was darker in the sun, because it was behind him, and his face was in shadow quite dark. . . .

He lifted her to her feet in one easy movement and slid his arms round her. There, with the sea lapping gently round their bodies, they kissed. He murmured something and they began to wade towards shore, slowly, feeling the pull of the water, as if it was trying to make them go back. But the swim was over, they had been in long enough.

They neared the car, erasing the old marks of their feet with newer, damper prints, and when they were nearly there he slid his arm up Isla's back and tugged gently at

28

her dark curls until she was forced to look up at him. Her heart was still beating rapidly from the last, salty, beautiful kiss. And this one was even better. Time ceased to matter as they clung to each other, the sun drying their backs, wet bodies held together, arms tightly round each other, and a kiss that went on and on, until. . . .

"My God!" he said, and pulled himself away and looked down at her, and his eyes had gone very dark. "My God, I think you'd better go and get in that car and change." They were both trembling, she knew she was, deep inside her, and she could see him, the fine tremor in his hands as he held her away from him. Their eyes met and held, but it was Isla who looked away first.

"All right," she said. "All right. Let me go." Her voice as husky as his had been, she could scarcely breathe. She knew how explosive the situation was, how potentially dangerous. One touch, one word. . . . Anything could happen. Then he released her, and she saw the white marks from his fingers on her arms, and turned away and stumbled to the car and pulled the towels out. One for him, one for her.

She waited until he had vanished behind the rock before she began to dry herself.

They were climbing now, the car in its lowest gear to take the sharp corners of the steep hill road. The dizzy panorama spread out behind them and Isla turned to look out of the rear window at the vast expanse of sea below them, miles away, and deep on the horizon the funnels of a boat coming into sight. The town was just visible when the road twisted a certain way, and it could have been miles away, so tiny did the buildings look, like matchbox toys.

The tension that had filled the car for a few minutes had vanished. They had both dried and changed, and Isla had called Kyle when she was ready, only her hair left, and this she was vigorously rubbing as he walked slowly towards her, holding his wrung out trunks in his left hand. He had reached out and touched her arm.

"I'm sorry, Isla," he had said.

She shook her head. "Don't – please," she said. "It's all right, Kyle." And she had smiled. They had got in, spread the suits out on the back ledge to dry and set off. Kyle looked at her, his face serious as he drove back along the white wide road.

"I promised to behave myself," he said, and gave a wry grin. "It won't happen again."

"I know." And gradually they both relaxed, so that now, as she looked at the shining view, it was easy to speak, to tell him how beautiful she thought it all was.

"It is. Wait until we get to George's."

"Who? George?" she began to laugh.

"What's so funny?" he demanded, trying to look stern.

The laughter was more than his words warranted, but it was a release from the last remaining shreds of tension for her. "Nothing," she said after a few moments. "Only it's such a nice ordinary name for this apparently fabulous place we're going to."

"I see. You have a point there. George is an old friend of mine. He's Greek – and what he can't do with food isn't worth knowing."

"Mmm, lovely," she sighed. "I'm starving!"

"You won't be when you've finished eating, I promise

you. You'll need a siesta."

"Somewhere in the shade, I hope."

"In the shade," he agreed. "There's a fabulous terrace with beach chairs on, you can stretch out and nobody will bother you."

"And what about you?" she asked.

He shrugged, not taking his eyes from the road, for the bends were trickier now, and steeper, and each twist and turn held its own surprises, with rocks, trees and shrubs seeming almost to be about to fall down on them. "I'll see. I might be too busy catching up on the news to bother resting."

"In Greek?" she asked, only joking.

"Of course!" he looked surprised.

She began to laugh. She had been impressed by his fluent Portuguese in Rio, both to Maria and her family, and at various restaurants they had visited. "Go on then, tell me how many languages you speak," she asked.

"Only six. What about you?"

"The usual. French and Latin, and I can make myself understood in Portuguese since coming over here –" and she hesitated, wondering if he would begin to ask any awkward questions. But he appeared not to notice.

"That's fair enough. We must have a conversation in French some time." And then he added abruptly: "Do you always speak to the boys in English?"

"Yes. Maria wants them to learn, for when they next go to England." Something was not quite right. But she couldn't put her finger on it. She didn't know what it was, this instinct that told her that there was something ever so

31

slightly wrong.

The moment passed; he made a comment about the scenery, a couple of cars passed them, and he had to slow down, as did the others, to enable them all to pass in safety. She soon forgot the slight unease she had felt at something said or unsaid. It had happened before, no doubt it would again, and there was nothing she could do about it, for some things could not be put into words, even if she had tried.

"There it is." His words broke into her thoughts. She looked ahead to a most English-looking mansion lying on a flat flower-crowded plateau in front of them. White-painted brick, it could have been a hotel anywhere in England, gracious, spacious, elegant – expensive.

"Yes, I see what you mean. I'm looking forward to meeting George," she admitted.

"Any minute now and you will." There were several cars parked at the front of the house, and a fountain twinkled coolly and prettily on the lawn beside them as Kyle parked the car. The palms were very tall and spiky and in the distance children shouted in play.

George was delighted to see Kyle. Short, fat and voluble, he greeted them with a beaming smile of welcome and drew them into the wide cool hall.

"You will sit, eh? Kyle, I have some wine –" he put two fingers and thumb to his mouth in an elaborate kiss, "I knew you would arrive soon. And then, when you have drunk, we will decide what you are to eat –"

He led the way in, and Kyle took Isla's arm as they followed him, and whispered:

"It's easier to let George have his own way – after all,

he should know what's best," and she nodded in agreement.

Quite a few people were seated eating, and the clatter of cutlery mingled with voices in a restful, unhurried atmosphere, as if time had ceased to matter while you were here. Isla looked round her as she seated herself at a table in a cool shady corner of the large room. One or two heads turned as they went in, and she saw one woman still staring at Kyle, who, because his back was to the room, seemed unaware of the scrutiny. Isla hid her smile as she bent to adjust the serviette on her knee. Not difficult to see why she was interested; he would turn heads in any room, the size and build and features of him. How strange, she thought suddenly, that we should have met as we did on the beach. If the baby hadn't strayed when he did. . . .

"You're away somewhere again." His deep voice was almost amused. Not quite. She smiled. "I was just thinking about the day we met, how if Marcos hadn't toddled off when he did, and you'd not been passing at that exact moment –" she stopped, surprised by what she saw in his face. "W–what is it?" She had expected him to laugh, to be amused, but a fleetingly grim expression, almost of anger, had crossed his face and was gone. Not quick enough – for she had seen.

Then he was shaking his head, smiling again, everything normal. She must have imagined it. She *must* have. "No, nothing," he assured her. "Nothing at all." But she wasn't sure if she believed him.

George was not only an attentive host, he was the perfect chef, and all the tiny niggling doubts of Isla's were gradually forgotten as the next hour passed in a golden glow of delicious food. She ate stuffed vine leaves for the first time in her life, and found them so delicious that Kyle had to warn her that if she ate too many she would have no room for other food. They were in a small silver bowl on the table, looking like green dates, deliciously stuffed with a savoury rice mixture, and after the third one she pushed the bowl to his side of the table. "All right – bully," she told him. "Take them. Don't let me have any more – I bet you only want them for yourself anyway," and she pulled a face, and he grinned at her.

"Of course. I'm a secret stuffed vine leaf addict," he admitted. And then George came with hors d'oeuvres, and there really was no more time to talk. Two hours later, stretched out on a deliciously comfortable lounging settee on a private terrace, Isla thought back over the meal, and the time just before they'd eaten when a chance remark had caused something she didn't understand; Kyle's near-anger. She could hear his voice now, distantly, talking to George in the kitchens of the hotel. They laughed often, the two men, the Greek and the Englishman, and it was pleasant to hear, and Isla closed her eyes, just for a moment or two as she listened.

When she woke the sun had moved, and a stray beam caught and dazzled her as she sat up, blinking. The leaves on the tree behind her shifted gently in a slight breeze, and the voices had stopped. There was silence now, no men talking, just the faint cry of distant birds high in the sky and the crick-crick of insects in the bushes nearby. Isla stood up and stretched. She had a sudden strange lost feeling inside her. For a moment it was as if she was all alone, there on a strange terrace, and Kyle gone away. . . .

"So you're awake." His voice was sudden and unexpected and she whirled round, face breaking into a happy smile as she went towards him.

"Kyle! For a moment I thought you'd gone." She reached out to touch his arm, not knowing why she was doing it, only that it was nice to see him.

"Gone? Without you? What a funny girl. You've been asleep for three hours." He looked down at her, and ran a finger down the side of her face, quite gently. "I've been talking to George. I came out once and you were dead to the world," he grinned. "So I went back to have a drink with George and one thing led to another." He looked at the recently vacated lounger with a wistful expression. "If I put my head down now I'd be off in a minute."

"Then why don't you?" she said. "There's a pile of magazines over there. I'll read for a while."

"And let me snore in peace?" He laughed. "That wouldn't be looking after you very well, would it?"

"I'll go for a walk instead. Really. After all I ate, and that sleep, I could do with some exercise anyway."

"No, I'll take you for a walk. You might get lost and that would never do." He took her arm. "Come on. There are some super views about a mile away. It'll give us an appetite for dinner."

"Are we eating here?" she asked.

"Don't you want to? George would be disappointed if you didn't."

"Why, yes, but I thought – haven't you got some business to do?"

He shrugged carelessly. "It can wait until morning. The day is too nice to worry about work. I can phone from here when we get back anyway, that'll do for a start. Come on."

There was no point in arguing; not that she wanted to. Isla picked up her white straw bag from the stone floor of the terrace and they set off down a leafy path that led into a forest of thick old trees. It grew rapidly cooler as the sunlight was cut off from them and she shivered slightly.

"We'll be out of here in a minute," he said, and put his arm round her shoulder. It was a casual, friendly gesture, nothing more to it than that, and yet Isla felt herself go warm, felt a pleasant glow at his touch. No man had ever affected her in the same way, not one, and yet this man, in less than two weeks, was having the strangest effect on her. She wondered, not for the first time, if she was falling in love with him. If this *was* love, it was good. It was a warmly agreeable, happy sensation, a desire to be near him – and she thought: I wonder if he's feeling the same? She looked at him briefly as they emerged from the shadow into sunlight. If he kept his arm on her shoulder – but he didn't. He took it away, looked down and grinned at her, almost as if reading her thoughts. "Happy?" he said.

"Yes. It's lovely here. Thank you for bringing me."

"Wait until later this evening. There's a nice surprise."

"What is it?"

"Wait and *see*," he teased. "It won't be a surprise if I tell you, will it?"

"Well – no," she agreed, as if reluctant. How pleasant

it was to be able to talk to someone like this, casual and friendly, yet with that warm undercurrent that she didn't always understand herself; only that she sensed he was aware of it too.

He took her along the path, and the air was heady and scented and warm. They were climbing slightly, the trees behind them now, the hotel still visible, but much smaller, the lawns surrounding it richly green.

"I like George," Isla said suddenly.

Kyle laughed. "He likes you too," he told her, amused. "If you'd heard what he said you'd have gone pink. Good job it was in Greek."

She shook her head softly. "I heard you talking before I fell asleep. When I woke up, it was all quiet." She turned to him. "Do you know – for a moment it seemed as if I was completely alone, as if you'd gone and left me." She smiled at the absurdity of it and looked into his eyes expecting to see his amusement. She heard his sharp intake of breath, and his face was hard for just that moment of time – then it was gone, and might never have been. But it had happened before – and now Isla knew it had not been her imagination. There was something about him at times that almost frightened her. It seemed impossible – yet it was so.

CHAPTER THREE

"IF I eat any more I won't be able to move," Isla protested. Everything was so different now. At night the hotel was a fairytale palace, floodlit, coloured lights strung across the trees, over the lawn, lending a magical air to the velvet black night. She looked around her and sighed in sheer contentment. They were dining out on the terrace, one of a few privileged tables, while inside the hotel the dining room was crowded. Here were five tables, each lit only by a red candle in a bottle, the soft glow making everything seem gold and unreal, and Kyle's face was gentle as she looked at him. Her heart gave a funny flip, almost of joy. Not only the place, the atmosphere was different too. It was as if he was exerting himself to be extra charming, as if he really *cared*. She was beginning to think that perhaps he did.

"You can manage a portion of *halva*," Kyle told her. "You must. George wants you to try it especially."

"Well –" she bit her lip. "It's that nougaty stuff, isn't it?"

"Nougaty stuff!" he nearly exploded into laughter. "Don't let him hear you. It's like describing caviare as a 'sort of fish'. No, Isla, try some – please."

"How can I refuse you?" she said lightly.

A waiter materialized at their side as if by magic. The soft murmur of voices from the other tables was echoed by an even fainter sound of music coming from the inside of the hotel. Everything was perfect, just perfect, thought Isla as she watched Kyle tell the young man – one of George's three sons – their order. There was a bottle of wine on their table. He lifted it as the youth disappeared, and poured some into Isla's glass.

"That's enough – really," she said faintly. "I'll be tipsy."

"Good, you'll be abe to dance better."

"Dance?" she echoed. "Where?"

"On the lawn, where else?"

"Oh!"

The *halva* was very sweet, quite delicious. The wine, and the coffee and liqueurs that followed, combined to give Isla a heady, light feeling, almost as if she were floating. It really was extraordinary, she thought, as they eventually walked away from the table towards the comparatively darker lawn, where couples were already dancing to the fascinating sounds of a group with steel drums. Really quite extraordinary, she could never have imagined enjoying herself so much, anywhere. She looked around her as they reached the edge of the lawn, and soft laughter came from nearby. Kyle took her in his arms. They had danced before, at a club he had taken her to, but this, out of doors, was different. The night air was softly caressing to her skin, faintly scented with the flowers which now slept, and there was so much less light that if he kissed her, no one would see. . . .

But he didn't. Not then, not at first. They danced for a while, and Isla stumbled once or twice, and he held her closer and whispered: "You're not *drunk*, are you?"

39

"I told you I would be if I had any more wine," she retorted, and he laughed softly.

"Never mind. You want me to carry you round?"

"You *dare* —" and then she remembered, and added hastily, "I mean no, thank you!"

The mood was just right, the music soft and enchanting, and nothing else seemed to matter except that moment in time, just the two of them together. The band vanished inside for a drink, couples stayed where they were talking, laughing, and Kyle said: "Let's go for a walk."

"Mustn't we be getting back to the town soon? It's gone twelve."

"The night is only just beginning. We're to go in for supper with George before we go," Kyle said as if surprised. "So if we go for a walk now, it should help to give us an appetite."

And without waiting for her assent, he took Isla's arm and began walking towards the darker trees, away from that brightly lit house, windows agleam with gold, leaving the noise behind until they were along a quiet shadowed path and when they were half way along it, he kissed her. It took Isla by surprise. One moment they were walking along slowly, the next he had stopped, pulled her round and turned her face up to his with one hand while the other held her firmly. A kiss ... that was all it was, a simple kiss, but there was such meaning and purpose to it that after the first startled moment Isla melted into his arms and was lost, caught in half-remembered memories, floating away on a warm tide of emotion, blissfully lost. ...

His voice was husky when he spoke: "Oh, Isla, Isla."

Tender fingers touched her face, caressing, gentle, and he stroked her lips, and she wondered if she would die of happiness, because nothing so wonderful had ever happened before.

"I think we'd better go back," he said, and she reached up to touch his cheek.

"No," she said softly. "Not yet." She stood on tiptoe because he was so tall, and kissed him, uncaring what he might think about that. She felt his arms tighten around her and a fleeting memory of how it had been on the beach came back to haunt her, but only for a second.

Then the kiss was over. She felt his fingers on hers, pulling her away from him, and he was looking down at her. "Yes, we'd better go back, Isla," he said, and something had changed, something in his voice that she didn't understand.

She stood quite still and looked up at him, and the darkness had a power of its own, because when it was night, everything was different – especially Kyle.

"All right, we'll go back," she agreed, and they began walking towards the light, and the people again. After that, everything was changed. Isla could not imagine in what way, but it was so. The fine careless magic was gone. They danced again, and after that went into George's private sitting room to meet his family, and a few other privileged friends – and it was very pleasant, everyone relaxed and friendly, and the drink flowed freely, and one of George's sons made it quite clear that if she had not been with Kyle, he would have pursued Isla relentlessly. Looking at Kyle, sitting in a corner talking to George, Isla had a brief temptation to try and make him jealous.

She was dancing past with Costas, the son, at the time, and it was difficult to keep him at a respectable distance. Kyle looked up at that moment, almost as if he had read her thoughts, and glanced briefly at her, then at the amorous Costas. His expression changed by only the merest flicker, but for some reason Costas almost immediately relaxed his hold on her, and when they were at the other end of the long room, away from Kyle and George, Costas whispered:

"I felt the knife then." She knew what he meant, but she pretended not to, because there was still a small hurt remaining from what had happened outside on that dark path.

"What do you mean?" It was easy to sound puzzled and amused. Costas was actually a very pleasant young man, as well as being darkly handsome.

"Your Kyle. I would not like to tangle with that one," a graceful shrug lightened the words.

"Oh!" She made it surprised. They had stopped dancing to stand by the open french windows that led out on to another part of the terrace. "Heavens, he's not 'my' Kyle at all."

"No?" There was polite disbelief in Costas' voice. "Never mind. You are with him, that is enough. Ah –" he gave an elaborate sigh, "if you were alone," and his dark liquid eyes melted hers with a smouldering glance full of meaning "ah, then!"

Isla laughed. "Oh, Costas, really! No wonder this place is crowded if you talk to all the girls like that."

He looked deeply hurt. "Me? You wound me deeply, Isla. Never have I met anyone like you before – never will

I again," and she would have sworn that there was a glint of tears in the dark eyes. She marvelled at his acting ability. He really believed what he was saying – now. Half an hour after she had left, she would be forgotten, she had no illusions about that. And yet – it was pleasantly flattering, a balm to the slight sense of rejection she could not dispel. Kyle had wanted to kiss her, and had done so – and then suddenly the mood had shattered, and he had change in that subtle way she still did not understand.

"Did you enjoy the day out, Isla?" Kyle's voice was an intrusion in her thoughts. They were speeding back through the black night towards the town, and George and his hotel were far behind them. It was nearly four in the morning, and quite possibly the party would still be on, but Isla had nearly been falling asleep, and Kyle had seen, and asked her if she wanted to leave.

It was the first time he had spoken since getting in the car. Isla had closed her eyes, and he had driven off in silence. She couldn't understand her own feelings; she was confused, uncertain, wanting in a way to hurt him – in another way to forget the slight incident in the garden.

"Yes, thanks. The food was absolutely super – George is a marvellous host."

"Yes, I know. You had an admirer too."

"Costas? He's very nice. And a good dancer." And she gave a little laugh, as if she could have said more, but had decided not to.

"So I noticed," was the dry reply, and his tone gave absolutely nothing away. Isla felt her fingers tighten helplessly on her bag. If he tried to kiss her when they went in, she would not let him, she decided.

He didn't. They crept along deserted dimly lit corridors until they reached their rooms and Kyle opened her door for her and handed her the key. "Goodnight, Isla, sleep well. I'll see you in the morning." And he was gone.

She heard his door shut quietly as she flung her bag on the bed. That was it. The day was over. She wondered why on earth she should want to cry.

The knock on the door woke Isla and she stumbled out of bed to undo the bolt, murmuring a drowsy: "Come in," before diving back under the cool sheets.

Kyle came in carrying a cup of coffee, which he set down on her bedside table.

"Good morning. Are you ready to travel yet?"

She looked sleepily at him. He looked disgustingly wide awake and healthy, his hair wet as if he had just been swimming, the pale blue shirt he wore unbuttoned, as if it were too warm to do up.

"Good morning. Thank you for the coffee. I will be when I've drunk it. What time is it?"

"Nearly eleven. I've been on the phone for a while, as well as having a quick dip in the pool. Would you like breakfast sent up to you here?"

She shook her head, then winced, because it still ached. "No, thanks — I couldn't eat for hours, after that food at George's. Where are we going?"

"Just to another island about two hundred miles away from here," but his voice was different as he said it, and she looked at him quickly. What on earth was it?

"I'll get ready now." And she waited for him to go,

44

heart fast beating. He turned and went out, closing the door quietly after him, leaving her alone with her thoughts. For a moment, as she sipped the coffee and watched a tiny spider crawling up the wall, Isla wondered if he regretted bringing her – and wondered too if she had made a mistake in coming. Everything was turning out so subtly different from what she imagined. In Rio they had been so happy together – at least she had – she was beginning to wonder now about him, how his manner of inscrutability had so often puzzled her, then been forgotten. She knew nothing about him, she was beginning to realize, absolutely nothing.

A bath might make her feel better. She put down the empty cup and went into the bathroom to run the water.

An hour later she was walking up the steps and into the plane. For a moment she turned and looked back at the island they would so soon leave behind. She heard Kyle's voice from the cockpit. "All right?"

"Yes, thanks." He came out then. She looked at him. It wasn't her imagination – he was completely different. A tall tanned stranger with sun-bleached hair and hard eyes – yes, that was it. His eyes, the mirrors of the soul, were different from anything she had ever seen in him. And for the first time since knowing him, she felt frightened of him. She turned away quickly, in case he should see, but he was busy checking everything before take-off, putting the steps away, closing the door, eyes travelling round the cabin in practised manner as if mentally noting everything.

"Fasten your seat belt, Isla. Can you manage?"

"Yes." She sat down and did as he told her and her

45

fingers trembled momentarily, but if he saw he gave no indication. Then she was alone, and could hear him in the cockpit, preparing for take-off, talking into the radio as he did so. She sat back and tried to relax, but her fingers curled round the ends of the arm-rests and tension filled her. She wished she had not come away with Kyle Quentin.

She had once read that storms can begin with frightening suddenness in the Caribbean. It was easy to read it – it was vastly different from the reality. It was several hours later. Quite suddenly the plane was plunged into darkness, and for a moment she felt only a blank surprise. Then she heard Kyle's voice calling her. "Come in here, Isla."

She obeyed, putting down the magazine she had been reading. She had not wanted to go in there. She felt, most oddly, as if she had nothing to say to him, and so she had stayed in the main cabin. Now, she obeyed the command in his voice. The cabin lights came on and flickered briefly before settling into a kind of dim glow, duller than they should be – almost frightening.

She went into the seat beside him. "Fasten your seat belt." He didn't need to tell her why. The evidence was all around them, not only the blue-green flashes of lightning which now crackled along the outside of the plane, but in the sudden blinding, *lashing* rain which obscured their vision and made it seem as if they were in the middle of a white, rushing waterfall. She looked at the face of the man beside her because now she was frightened, very frightened, and she needed reassurance. . . .

She wouldn't speak to him. Concentration was in every line, in every slight movement that he made, and she dared not disturb him. But I trust him, she thought suddenly. It's strange, but just now, looking at him, I'm not frightened any more. And she wasn't. There was something about him that dispelled the fearful tension that had filled her, a kind of sureness that took no heed of the bucketing movements of that small craft. Despite everything, incredibly, he was in control of the plane.

There was a searing, blinding flash, a roar – and almost immediately after, the smell of burning, faint yet ominous. She dared not speak – but Kyle did. "Looks like an engine's gone," he said. "I'm going to try and land. I'm going to get down fast, so for God's sake hold on to your seat."

She did. The sickening sensation that followed, as if of being in a giant lift that had gone mad and was plummeting to earth, *was* frightening, but he was doing it deliberately, as he told her only seconds later. It was to get under the storm, to be able to see an island to land, anywhere now, for if they hadn't been blown too much off course, and if the light was not too obscure, there should be an island that had a landing strip. Then she prayed – prayed that they would find this place, and she trembled as she held tight to her seat, and wondered what was going on in Kyle's mind – whether he was frightened too.

The next few minutes were a nightmare, a kaleidoscope of sound and lights and the ever-present rain, which mercifully was less and less as they neared the sea, skimming along over the waves, buffeted by winds, the air inside the cabin deathly cold and chill, as if. . . .

"Right. Thank God!" And the words were almost like a prayer as Isla saw it rushing to meet them – trees and shrubs and white sand, then he was banking, turning to approach it at a better angle, and she closed her eyes because this was something she didn't want to see. She had reached the limit of her strength. Everything that happened now was like a dream – or a nightmare, a living, noisy nightmare, and she wanted to scream. . . .

Falling, falling, tumbling into blackness, and it was soft and warm now, and there was no pain, only a dull jagged ache in her head, but it didn't seem to matter any more. . . .

"Isla! We're safe. Isla, wake up – wake up!"

The voice came from a great distance, then nearer and less echoing until it gradually focussed into Kyle's, and Isla opened her eyes. She was in some sort of shed – for a minute she thought it was still the plane, and she struggled to sit up, and found she had been lying on the floor, and her head ached terribly.

"Kyle!" she said. "Where are we?"

"We're safe. We're on an island whose name I can't for the life of me remember, and you're sitting on the floor of the Nissen hut that once served as airport building."

She looked round her then. It was dark, so that Kyle was a grey shadowy blur beside her, kneeling down, and she could hear the rain drumming on the tin roof in a violent tattoo, lashing down the windows, and Isla shivered.

"The plane – is it –" she stopped.

"I don't know yet. I had to get us out first. There's

no fire – I got that out with an extinguisher and the rain did the rest, but the plane is damaged. How much I'll have to wait until morning to see."

"Oh, Kyle! How awful – and how marvellous you were to bring us down safely." She put her hand to her forehead, because something about it bothered her, then she winced.

"Don't. You banged your head. Now you're okay I'll put something on. You'll live," he finished, and she could almost see the grin on his face. The slight tension, the feeling of hurt at what had happened the previous night were all washed away with what had happened since.

"You were wonderful, Kyle," she said. "I was never even frightened – well, only towards the end – but I never doubted your ability to get us out, if it was humanly possible."

"Didn't you?" He got to his feet in a graceful, easy movement and pulled Isla to hers. "I wish you'd told *me* – I was scared stiff."

She shook her head. "No, you weren't. I could tell. That's what made me calmer." She began to shiver. It was cold and she wore only a thin cotton dress, and it was soaked.

"You're suffering from shock. Listen, I'm going to get as much as I can from the plane. There are travelling rugs too – I'll fetch those."

"I'll come with you," she said promptly. "I can carry anything you want." She saw his doubtful expression only faintly in the dark. "Please," she begged. "Let me do something."

"All right. Come on." He took her hand and they ran

out into the rain, along weed-covered concrete with water bouncing upwards with the force of the drops, feeling it coursing down her face and back, and knowing that they were *safe*.

That was the best thing of all, that made everything else seem unimportant. They were safe. Where didn't matter, and there was time to worry about the implications of their plight later. They were alive, and that was all that mattered.

Her breath caught in her throat when she saw the plane slewed across the end of the airstrip at a disturbing angle. Gone the trim craft she remembered. This was a pathetic creature with a broken look about it; an almost drunken air.

Kyle leapt up nimbly and leaned down to pull Isla up after him into the sloping-floored cabin which had a ghostly deserted air about it.

"I'll throw our cases out," he said. "You get the blankets out of the lockers," and he pointed. "Then we'll take enough food to eat for now. The rest can wait until morning."

The next few minutes were too busy to talk. With plastic sheeting over their heads and shoulders they walked back to the Nissen hut piled up with all they could carry, careful not to allow the blankets to get wet.

Fifteen minutes later, soup was bubbling on a stove, and Isla was steaming herself gently dry in front of it, blanket-wrapped, her clothes spread out on a bench to dry. Kyle, his blanket draped over him like a Roman toga, was stirring the soup. Isla looked up at him and laughed in sheer relief. "All the comforts of home," she said.

"We are having coffee and liqueurs afterwards, aren't we?"

"Coffee and liqueurs, madame?" Kyle removed the spoon from the soup with a flourish. "Coffee, yes – liqueurs, I regret, no – except, hey, there's some brandy in the galley. How about that?"

She shook her head faintly. "I don't believe it! And I was only joking!"

"Never mind. I'd forgotten. Brandy might do you good. I don't want you fainting all over the place."

"I won't faint, don't worry." Her tone was decisive.

She saw the shrewd look he gave her. "No, I don't think you will. Okay, we'll forget the brandy for now. Let's get this down us instead." They had carried all they reckoned they might need in a large plastic bag. It had been difficult getting everything out of the plane; the floor sloped at a dizzy angle, and it had been necessary to hold on at every step, to lean on seats and cling to the backs of them. The effort was worthwhile, for the hot chicken soup, drunk out of thick beakers, was delicious, and just what Isla needed to restore her strength. Afterwards they drank coffee, and had a cigarette.

"Where are we going to sleep?" Isla had the sudden thought and looked round her at the shadowy shed, only the ancient stove in front of them throwing out a faint light, but not enough to see anything of their surroundings.

"We could try on the plane for tonight, until I can fix something up. It'll be more comfortable."

Something in his words touched a chord of unease within her. "Until you can fix something up," she repeated. "Kyle — how long are we g-going to be here?" There was silence for a moment. Then he spoke. "Do you want an honest answer?"

"Yes." Her hand tightened on her coffee cup. "Of course I do."

"Then I don't know. I'd like to say — no time at all, but I can't. The radio is bust and I'm not sure if I can mend it — and we're about a hundred miles off course. This island is right off the beaten track. If they think we've gone down in the sea, they'll make a good search — and then that'll be that."

"You mean —" she could hardly say the words, "you mean nobody w-will be looking for us?"

"No."

"Oh, God!" The cry was wrung from her.

"Listen. It's dark, it's chucking it down. Things always seem worse at night — you should know that. When morning comes we'll start thinking about everything. You never know, I might even be able to fix the radio. If I can — well, if *not* — then we'll think of something, don't worry." He leaned over and grasped her arm, and the gesture was very comforting.

She slept eventually, but her sleep was full of terrifying dreams. One was so vivid that it woke her up and she lay there, eyes wide with fear, until she remembered where she was and sat up very cautiously. The plane was at such an angle that Isla was virtually jammed up against the side of it as she lay on the reclining seat. The blanket had fallen off her and she leaned over to pick it up and saw Kyle in the seat behind her cocooned in his rug, fast asleep.

She smiled faintly to herself. He looked as if he could sleep anywhere and not waken for anything. There was no sound of rain any more, and faint light filtered in through the portholes, lending an eerie greyness to the inside of the cabin. Everywhere was still and silent and Isla gradually relaxed again. Soon it would be morning. There were so many things to think about, but she would not allow herself to do so until morning arrived. Kyle had been right. Night time did make problems loom larger; in the sunlight, thought would come more clearly.

She breathed deeply and slowly, consciously making her aching body relax. There had been no embarrassment at having to share the sleeping quarters – she had not imagined that there would be. After supper was over both had put on dry clothes from their suitcases; Kyle a pair of jeans and sweater, Isla her trim blue pyjamas – far less revealing than a sun-suit, and sensible. She had felt only slightly self-conscious at first, but the feeling soon passed in the run across the wet tarmac, both sheltering under a huge sheet of plastic. Gradually her eyes grew heavy again, and she closed them. Her last thought before falling asleep again was that she had no idea how large the island was, or what it looked like in sunlight. She would soon know, she thought, in blurred fashion, as sleep overcame her.

"Isla! The sun is shining. It's a beautiful day again." Kyle's voice was rousing her gently from sleep, together with his hand on her arm. She looked up slowly, blinked and yawned, aware of her tousled hair and sleepy eyes. And then she smiled.

"Hello. How long have you been up?"

"Just a few minutes. I'm starving. I'm going to rustle up some food for us. Do you want to go along to the shed to get dressed?"

"Yes, I will." She began to sit up.

"And later we'll go round and see if there's any fresh water on the island. Until we do, don't use any in the galley, will you?"

She looked at him. She hadn't thought of that. Her mouth went dry at the thought. "You mean –" she had to swallow, "there may not be any?"

"I'll be surprised if there isn't – but don't look so worried, if the worst comes to the worst I'll rig up something to evaporate sea water. Go *on*, there's a good girl." And he turned away and began making a slow way to the galley. Isla scrambled out of her bed, leaned forward well to enable her to balance, and reached the door.

Their cases were on the bench in the Nissen hut. She changed into her cool yellow dress and sandals and put her pyjamas away. She walked more slowly back to the plane, looking round her for the first time. The long grey strip of runway had nearly been taken over by weeds; it was a wonder Kyle had landed on it so accurately. To her left the white sand stretched away until it reached the water. To her right was a dense mass of shrubs and trees, some of them tall palms towering above the rest, others shorter, all very green and lush-looking, as if the previous night's rain had brought new life and vigour to them. Steam rose from the puddles of rain on the concrete in front of Isla, and soon they would have disappeared altogether. It brought back Kyle's words to her. She had never appreciated just how precious water was before. His casual remark had jolted her into realization of their position. Yet she didn't doubt that if he had to, he would find some way of getting them a limited supply. She had the suddenly comfortable feeling that whatever the situation, he would provide.

They ate tinned sausages for their first meal of the day, drank coffee afterwards, and then Kyle said: "Come on, we're going to explore." He carried the empty tin, well cleaned out with a tissue, and she asked him why.

"Because if – *when* – we find that fresh water, we'll have a drink," he laughed. He helped her down from the plane, and for a moment his arms were round her waist in a firm decisive grip. Then he took them away and they walked round to the other side of the plane. Isla saw the fallen tree for the first time and stopped in her tracks. "We didn't hit this, did we?" she asked slowly.

"We did. If we hadn't the radio would be fine – I had a go at it before you woke, by the way, and it's dead. The storm must have blown it down. That was when you were jerked forward and knocked yourself." She felt suddenly sick, aware how close disaster had been, how cool he had kept, and she had not even imagined. . . .

"Oh, Kyle," she said, "you were wonderful – truly. What can I say to thank you?"

"Nothing." He grinned. "Nothing is needed." But the grin wasn't quite as cheerful as usual, and she wondered briefly if he was upset too. She couldn't even guess at what was in his mind, she could not even imagine just how soon she would find out. . . .

At the top of a small hill they found rocks and a tumbling spring of icy cold fresh water bubbling from the centre of the pile. They both knelt to splash it over their skin, and Kyle filled the tin with water and handed it to Isla.

"Thanks. I wonder if this is the fountain of youth," she said, smiling. "Just think, we could make a fortune selling maps of how to get here when we return to Rio –" and then she stopped, because Kyle's expression had changed; had become almost grim, quite suddenly. "Kyle, what – what is it?" she faltered, and a dreadful, *awful* feeling seized her, though she couldn't imagine why.

"Isla, I've got something to tell you," he began. "I suppose now is as good a time as any."

She could hardly breathe. Something dreadful was about to happen and she could do nothing to prevent it. She shook her head faintly, the tin held in her hand still full of untasted water.

"You know we met on Copacabana beach?" he asked her.

"Yes?" What was coming?

"It wasn't accidental, that meeting." He paused for a moment, and when he continued, his voice had become harsh. "I didn't just happen into your life, Isla. I was sent there – and paid for it – by your father. He's hired me to get you home to England, by any means I choose."

CHAPTER FOUR

SHE didn't believe him. How could she? Words like that are too dreadful to be true. They seemed to echo and reverberate in that space between them as they stood facing each other, and there was a quality of unreality about them. But then she looked at him properly, and his hard eyes told her all she needed to know.

Isla shook her head softly. "Oh no, oh no," and when he moved slightly towards her, she said: "No – don't come near me." She flung the tin to the ground and saw the water spill out to be swallowed by the greedy parched earth. Then she turned and ran down towards the beach, towards the safety and shelter of the Nissen hut.

It was baking hot inside there, but she didn't notice. She stood just inside the door, and she was trembling. She put her hand to her mouth and pressed it hard against her lips. But she wasn't going to cry – the shock went too deep for that. She heard his steps outside, felt the door being pushed open, and moved away.

"All right," he said. "I didn't intend to break it to you quite so bluntly –"

She found her voice. "Why have you told me?" she asked, and was quite surprised to find that she could speak in even tones. Because in a way, it was almost as if all this was happening to someone else.

She saw a muscle move in his dark tanned jaw. "Because I don't know how long we'll be stuck here, and I can't go on living a lie," he answered.

"You were going to take me back to England?"

"Yes."

A spark of anger lit her eyes. "Then perhaps it's a good thing for me that we crashed, isn't it?" She moved towards him, just a fraction. "If it's your plane I'm glad that it's damaged – *glad*." Then a thought struck her. "Or is it my father's? That would be funny!" She tried to laugh, but what came out was almost a sob. "Did he lend it to you? Did he pay you well?" Her voice was rising, and she watched him standing there in front of her, a giant of a man she had imagined she might be falling in love with – once. So long ago – so very long ago now. Just a few brief hours since their day on Trintero, but a yawning world of time away now that his words had been spoken.

"It's my plane, not your father's," he said. It was his calm manner that Isla found more wounding than anything else. She felt as if she wanted to get through it. But how? She wanted to hurt him as much as he had just hurt her, but there was no way. Had she ever thought him a pleasant, gentle man? What a fool she had been!

Under that calm exterior he was all steel, hard and implacable – and utterly hateful. Isla was breathing hard now. The air in the hut was stifling her, she felt as if she couldn't breathe. And they were here, just the two of them – and for how long? The idea of spending any more time in his company was utterly unbearable.

"I think I *hate* you," she said in a loud clear voice, just so that there could be no mistake.

"I know," he answered. "But you'll get over it. We're

here, and we've got to get it organized if we're to be comfortable, so I suggest we talk things over. The first thing is to get out of this shed before you faint from the heat." Sweat beaded his brow and ran down his face, and Isla watched him, as he opened the door and waited for her to go out.

"I'm going to change and go for a swim," she said. "So why don't *you* go out if you can't stand the heat in here?"

"All right if you stay in the shallow water," he answered. "There are sharks here, and they're not fussy who they eat."

"And you wouldn't like that, would you?" she retorted. "Having no goods to deliver, I mean? What *would* Daddy say then?" And as he turned to go out, clearly with no intention of responding to her taunt, she added: "And you wouldn't get *paid* either, would you?" He closed the door. He had gone. She went over to her suitcase and pulled out her yellow swimsuit. A small feeling of triumph filled her, short-lived, gone almost instantly, but it had existed. Her barbed remark had reached him, as she had intended. His reaction had only been slight, but enough to let her see that he wasn't as impregnable as she imagined.

As she pulled the swimsuit on she thought back to their first meeting on Copacabana beach. How accidental, how very casual it had seemed. She had swallowed the bait, been beautifully landed – literally, for here she was, with him. How skilfully he had acted the part, she thought bitterly, seeing again his face on the occasions he had come into the apartment, the quiet mannerly air that had so captivated Maria and her children – and Isla herself.

"Oh yes," she said quietly as she wriggled into the skin-tight suit, "I fell for it all right. Nearly fell for you too, Mr. Quentin." And hot tears scalded her eyes and she blinked them away quickly. So he was going to take her back to England, was he? "That's what you think!" she said softly, and went out of the shed, leaving the door open. There was no sign of Kyle. The airstrip and sand were deserted and silent, and it was almost eerie. She looked towards the plane. He could be aboard, trying to mend the radio again, checking the extent of the damage. Isla ran across the baking hot concrete briefly regretting leaving her sandals off, but without sufficient energy to run back for them to the shed.

She went into the water, and it was warm in the first few shallow steps, then cooler as it grew deeper. She plunged forward and swam outwards, revelling in the cool saltiness on her warm skin. When she came out she would wash her previous day's clothes at the spring, and they would be dry in no time. She turned and floated on her back, and the sun hit her wet face, drying it instantly, leaving a salty taste on her lips. But how, she wondered, would she be able to keep out of Kyle's way? A nightmare prospect suddenly came to her, of them being stranded for weeks, even months, just the two of them on the island, and she took a deep breath and thought about that for a moment, and was filled by a cold sick sensation.

If only it were not true! If only he was just what she had thought at first, a marvellous, attractive man she was growing to like very much. If. . . . But there was no going back now. The words, the dreadful words, had been spoken, and in those few minutes everything had changed, and nothing would ever be the same again. For Isla had trusted him, had thought she had met the first real man in her young life – and the betrayal was all the greater because of that. He had hurt her too deeply, more than he would ever imagine, or even care. For she had seen his eyes. The hardness she had occasionally glimpsed no longer puzzled her. Now she knew him for what he was. She would never trust him again.

"Isla, come out now," his voice commanded, and she turned away, ignoring it, and struck out away from the shore in a gesture of childish defiance. She was still in fairly shallow water, and he was worse than any sharks.

"*Isla!* Can you hear me?" His voice was louder, no anger in it. Was he, she wondered idly, as she kicked out, ever angry? A mood of recklessness filled her. What would he do if she went out further and further? The private misery inside her was stronger than any fear of him, or of what he might say or do. Isla swam idly, apparently indifferent to anything, yet with one eye open for the sight of a familiar fin. The shock of his words had worn off now, she was tired of thinking about them. One thing that life with her father had taught her was how easy it is to erect an emotional barrier against hurt and disappointment in life. Living as she had done under his dominating power, her friends chosen for her, unsuitable ones quietly and skilfully made to realize they weren't welcome, had helped Isla to become harder – or at least to appear so. That was why the last three months had been so glorious; so happy and carefree – until now. Kyle had spoilt it all.

Maria would be worried, as would Roberto and the boys. Dear Maria, with her concern for Isla. She blinked hard. No use worrying about them now, she could do nothing to let them know. . . .

"For God's sake come on in!" Kyle's voice startled her so that she swallowed some water and spluttered it out violently. He was treading water beside her. She turned on him.

"Why should I? Go away!"

"I told you not to go far out. You've reached the limit. There *are* sharks, I'm not joking, I'm serious. Now are you coming out of the water on your own or do I take you out?"

She gave him a level stare. "I'd prefer it if you didn't touch me." His eyes were as hard as tempered steel as they met hers, and for a moment the glances clashed and held.

"Then get going," he suggested softly.

For the first time, Isla felt frightened of what would happen if he touched her. She turned suddenly from him and struck out for shore, and he swam beside her.

She shivered as she left the water, but only for a moment, for the sun's heat was on her immediately, drying the salty water, prickling her skin, turning it to gold.

She walked away from him, went into the Nissen hut and dug out the bar of soap from her suitcase, picked up her clothes from the bench and slipped on her sandals.

He was waiting outside, presumably for her to get

changed before he did so himself. She looked at him, at the dripping wet trousers he wore, and smiled faintly. "It's all yours," she told him. "I'm going to wash my clothes at the spring." And she walked away, tall, slender and beautiful, looking as if she didn't give a damn for him or anyone. He stood and watched her go, and his expression was unreadable.

The sheer physical work of soaping and rubbing the material of her dress and undies helped to ease some of the tension that inexplicably filled Isla. She couldn't understand herself. Later, when she was alone, she would think about it. Just now she did not want to.

She carried the clean dripping clothes down with her to the airstrip. There were some large leafy bushes near the hut. Her things would dry in no time at all in the hot sun, she knew. Already her mind was adjusting to the new situation of being stranded on a deserted island. It was also beginning to accept the fact that Kyle was a hypocrite – the worst kind – a man who would pretend affection for ulterior motives; in his case money.

How odd, she reflected as she spread her dress out carefully over a succulent-leaved flowering shrub, she had thought him to be the first man she had ever met who did not know of her father's wealth, and who therefore liked her for herself. How wrong can you be? she thought wryly, and had to swallow rather quickly. A dislike for him was growing slowly but surely within her with each hour that passed. She very deliberately put the treacherous, heart-stopping memory of his kisses out of her mind.

That would do her no good at all, to think of the nice things. The sooner she could see him as he really was, the better would she be able to win the battle. For she had no intention of returning to England, with or without him – particularly with him.

She heard the sound of banging from the direction of the plane. What was he doing? Not that she cared. The clothes were spread out, steaming gently with the heat, and Isla's swimsuit was already dry on her, and warm. She ran her fingers through her short curly hair. What now? There was really no choice. She walked slowly and reluctantly along the concrete, sandals on her feet now; she would not leave them off again.

He wasn't in the plane; he was outside, round at the back of it, and beside him on the sand were leafy branches, piled up. For a moment she considered the idea that he might be going to light a fire. If so, it was a foolish place. He saw the direction of her glance. "I'm camouflaging the petrol tanks with these twigs, to keep the sun off," he said. "So I advise you to stand away – you might get caught by the branches." His voice was quite expressionless, disinterested.

"Let me help you." She didn't know why she should say it. She wanted as little as possible to do with him.

"If you like. Though you'll get dusty –"

"Do you think I *care*?" Her eyes met his. "I've got to do something. If I sit around I might start thinking about why I'm here," and she didn't trouble to hide the bitterness behind the words.

Kyle slowly straightened up. "There's plenty to do, I can assure you," he answered. "But we'll do this job first. Then think about food and shelter. And self-pity won't do you any good at all."

"Self-pity?" Isla's voice rose slightly. "Do I sound sorry for myself? I assure you I'm not. I'm sorry for you, if you must know, having to do the kind of dirty work you must enjoy – or you wouldn't do it, would you? Unless it's the *money*," she deliberately emphasised the last word, and saw his face tighten, the muscles go taut in his cheek.

He said, and his voice remained quite quiet, "I don't intend to argue with you, so you're wasting your time, Isla. Save your energy for work instead of wasting it on me."

She took a deep breath, hating him for his calmness. What was there about him that could so infuriate her? So uninvolved. Didn't he know what he had done? Or didn't he care? She bent down and picked up a large leafy branch. The wood was dry and brittle feeling in her hand, the leaves already withering in the heat. He had been busy while she had been washing her clothes. Tension vibrated in the air around them, and she knew suddenly that he was not as unmoved as he seemed. She could sense it, could feel it as surely as if he had told her, and she felt her heartbeats quicken. Good!

And already in her mind, as yet vague and amorphous, a small plan stirred and began to take shape. She turned away, not wanting him to see her face, for he had a disconcerting habit of reading her thoughts, she had already discovered. But nothing would chase it away now; she was going to make him suffer for what he had done. How, she wasn't yet sure.

He took two branches and hefted them up to drag along, and Isla followed. He laid them against the side of the plane, and she did the same. There were many to bring, but it was done eventually, and Isla brushed herself down and looked ruefully at her dusty swimsuit. Kyle had taken his shirt off, and changed into his jeans and espadrilles. There was no doubt about his strength; it was evident in the effortless way he moved thick heavy branches, in the movement of powerful arm and chest muscles. Nor did he tire. Isla's arms trembled with the effort, but she was determined not to let him see. And she was very thirsty.

"Can we drink the water from the galley yet?" she asked him as they moved round to the door of the plane.

"No need. I'm going to fill two water containers from the spring. That will be much fresher." She looked at him.

"You do that. Meanwhile I'll make myself an orange drink." And she braced her arms, ready to climb in, and Kyle put his hands on her waist. Sudden anger and dismay flared in her and she wrenched his fingers viciously away and turned on him.

"When I want your help – I'll ask," she spat out. "Until then – *don't* touch me!" Her blue eyes blazed, her bosom heaved, and her hands clenched with the effort it cost her not to hit him.

"Grow up," he said, and his deep voice had a note in it that should have warned her. "You won't get anywhere with me with that behaviour. This isn't a big city, you know. The sooner you realize that, the better. We'll live by our own wits and intelligence – and how well we manage depends on us both pulling together, not fighting all the time."

"Fighting? I wouldn't know where to start with you. I'll bet you know all the dirty tricks in the book," she retorted. She sensed his equally rising temper, and it would be interesting to see just how far she could go before he lost it. It was like the build-up before a storm; the atmosphere charged and heavy. Something sparked between them and she felt reckless, uncaring of anything save the desire to hurt him. "You certainly played it dirty in Rio, didn't you? Why, I imagined you actually liked me!"

Her eyes widened with the effort to keep a treacherous tear back. "That was a silly thing for me to do, wasn't it? Anything – anyone – connected with m-my father is bound to be tainted. That's what too much money does for you." She faced him and her slender body trembled, but she had to go on now that she had started. He stood very still, then, quite suddenly, at her last words, he turned away as if he didn't want to listen to her any more. But Isla was too tensed up just to let it go at that. She did something she would never normally dream of doing – she reached out and grabbed his arm and tried to jerk him round.

"What's the matter? Afraid of the truth?" she taunted. He stood there and looked down at his arm, then at her, and his eyes had a dark look to them that made her catch her breath.

"I'm not afraid of anything – or anyone," he answered. "Least of all you. But I've got jobs to do. And I've already told you, I don't intend to argue or fight with you." As he spoke, Isla took her hands away from his arm, because she didn't really want to have to touch him, it had been an impulse.

67

Without another word she turned away and scrambled into the plane. Safely inside, out of his sight, she stood trembling for a moment, leaning against a seat for support. Then an odd thing happened. There was a strange creaking noise, and the plane lurched, nearly sending her sprawling. Then it settled, and was now listing at an even greater angle, so that it was virtually impossible to walk

She heard his voice from outside: "Isla? Are you all right?" but was too shaken to answer. The next moment she heard him come in, and half turned to look at him.

"It lurched," she said. "There was a funny noise — and then this happened."

"I saw it. You'd better get out. It may move further."

"I'm getting a drink first." She had set her heart on it, and she was even more thirsty now, than before.

"I'll get it out for you. Go outside."

"Go to hell!" She took the first tentative steps towards the galley, holding tight to the seats as she went. She was suddenly grabbed by Kyle, and felt his overpowering strength as he lifted her, leaning hard, went over to the door and dropped her down to the ground, jumping after her immediately, and beginning: "Listen — when I tell you to do something —"

Isla had reached the utter limit. To be ignominiously *bundled* out like a parcel had been the very last straw. She lashed out and caught him a stinging slap across the face. Then she stood there, legs trembling, her breath catching in her throat at the sight of him. She had wanted to see him angry. She had her wish. But she wasn't going to run, for where was there to go, to get away from *him*?

His eyes sparked fire, his voice shook as he said: "My

God, but you're pushing it a bit, aren't you? What makes you think I won't hit you back?"

Her chin tilted defiantly. "It wouldn't surprise me at all," she managed to get out. "In fact nothing about you would surprise me. Go ahead – I don't care."

"Don't tempt me," he grated. "It's a pity you weren't spanked when you were younger. You might have been less bloody spoilt now." The mark was fading on his face. She found she was watching it with an abstracted interest. He needed a shave too. Funny how dark the stubble was in contrast to the sun-bleached hair. Perhaps he dyed it . . . she repressed a giggle at the thought, and he reached out and held her arms just above the elbows and shook her, not roughly, not gently either.

"I've just about reached the end of my patience with you," he snapped. "I told you to get out of the plane because it could have tilted even more, any second, and you could have gone flying and cracked your head open. But you knew better, didn't you? So let's get one thing straight, *right now*. While we're here, I'm in charge, and what I say goes. Do you understand?"

Suddenly Isla's defiance evaporated. It was a combination of several things; the heat, tiredness, thirst – and although she would never admit it even to herself, fear of her own weakness against this bad-tempered giant of a man. She looked down, fighting back the sudden tears that threatened to overwhelm her.

"Do you understand?" he repeated, but she couldn't answer now. She looked up, and her eyes were swimming with the unshed tears.

Silently she nodded, and the tears spilled out and ran

down her cheeks. Her body shook with sobs. She didn'
see his face change, nor the expression that came over i
as he looked at her. She couldn't see anything except a
golden hazy blur, and couldn't feel anything except hi
warm hands on her arms, stopping her from falling.

"Oh, Isla," he said, but she scarcely heard the word
in her distress. She shook herself free from him and
turned away, to run towards the water, kneel down and
splash her face in that cool refreshing saltiness. She felt
better immediately afterwards, and stood up, intending
to go to the spring herself for water. Kyle could hardly
stop her doing that, she reasoned. But he was waiting for
her, by the plane when she went back, holding two beakers, by his feet two plastic water containers.

He held out one of the mugs. "I've made an orange
drink," he told her.

"Thank you." She took it from him and drank it
thirstily.

"I'm going up for water to the spring. Then I'm going
to see what fruit and vegetables are growing here, then
I'll try and catch a fish for lunch. We might as well save
the tinned food." He spoke in a completely impersonal
tone, as if they were strangers. Perhaps, she thought, it
was better that way. Less wearing on the nerves.

"Can I come with you to look for food?" she asked.
"I can't just do nothing."

"If you wish. While I'm gone for water, will you
search for twigs? We're going to have to light a fire. The
more fuel we get the better."

"Yes." She watched him walk away, after putting his
beaker down beside the plane. He strode off without a

70

backward glance and vanished into the green blackness of the trees. Isla bit her lip. So this was how it was going to be. A small shiver ran down her spine. The longer they spent together, the harder he seemed. More and more she was coming to see what a clever act he must have been putting on in Rio – and even on Trintero island. The thoughts made her feel almost ill. How gullible she had been, how foolish! And how he must have been laughing inwardly at her. That was what really hurt – to know that the affection to which her starved heart had so willingly responded had been a sham. She would not be able to forgive that.

She began to look for twigs and small branches. Any activity was better than none, and it was a challenge to see how well she could do before he came back from the spring. Once started the pile soon grew on the concrete, and Isla was just coming out of the trees, her arms full, when she saw Kyle walking towards her. Her heart skipped a beat. She couldn't help it; there was something very attractive – despite all his actions – that could not be denied. A big magnificent animal, that was how he seemed, carrying the two full water containers easily and lightly. Broad-shouldered, slim-hipped, he came nearer, and he watched her, and she had the chilling impression of a tiger ready to pounce, a brooding, waiting tiger that would show no mercy to its victim.

"I'm putting these near the hut. We won't be able to use the plane any more."

"Then where will we sleep tonight?"

He put the water containers down and straightened up. "Where do you suggest?" There was nothing in his tone she could take objection to, and yet Isla bit her lip. It seemed to imply that he wanted no more scenes, so she should be humoured. She followed his example and laid her pile of branches and twigs down, near to the waiting heap.

"I don't know. Out in the open?" Because I don't intend to stay in the hut with *you*, she added inwardly – but only inwardly. There had been enough anger gathered for one day, and his mood still seemed uncertain – unfathomable to her.

"There may be snakes. We'll have to see when we look for food. But otherwise there's no reason why not." He looked down at her collection of wood. "Leave that now, we can see to it later."

"All right." She couldn't understand why she was so ready to agree with him. Half an hour previously it had been very different. She still felt weak from their violent clash, and wondered what effect, if any, it had had on him. Probably none, she thought wryly as she followed him towards the Nissen hut. A man that hard would not be affected by a quarrel.

He had told her that he was in charge – that was the end of the matter. A helpless feeling swept over her. How could she fight *him*? There seemed no way, no way at all.

He carried a stick, and he went first. Isla followed him into the thick trees behind the Nissen hut, knowing that it was simply common sense, that he knew places like this far better than her, presumably, and that if he was any sort of man at all, he would hardly expose her to any danger by letting her go first into dense undergrowth.

The trees were suffocatingly close. No sunlight pene-rated here, all was darkness and shadow, and Isla felt an unreasonable surge of fear. For the first time since her discovery of Kyle's real character, she was thankful that he was near. To walk through this at night was unthinkable, for even now there was a dank eeriness all about them. Distant, faint cracklings and snappings indicated other creatures. Human or animal?

"Could there be anyone else living on this place?" She felt compelled to ask, even though she had not intended to speak, except where necessary.

"No. Not now," was the rather cryptic answer. She was soon to discover what it meant. They were climbing steadily, as well as having to push aside the thick green leaves and branches, and Isla took a deep breath. It was impossible to go quickly, but it was tiring in the heat, and she wondered how soon they would reach their destination, for something had already told her that there was a purposefulness to Kyle's walking. This was no aimless wandering for food; it was as if he knew where he was going. A distant bird cry seemed to hang in the air for moments after it had been shrilly uttered. Distant, even fainter cracklings in the very woods in which they stood told of other creatures. But what? Suffocating sudden panic filled her. It could be anything moving back there, anything at all – and Kyle seemed unaware of it. She wanted to tell him she was afraid, but didn't. It was sufficient for the moment that he was *there*. That was all. It grew lighter, the trees thinned, sunlight became stronger, and they emerged from the eerie greenness into a clearing. And there, set in the centre of that clearing, was a large house – or rather the remains of one.

CHAPTER FIVE

ISLA stood very still. Of all the things she had expected to see, a house had not even entered her mind. Kyle, as aware of her astonishment, waited without saying anything. The house had been built originally of a kind of reddish wood, single-storeyed, long, low, and rambling, with a verandah running the entire length of the front. Had been. Now the roof was gone, and part of the walls demolished perhaps by storms, with the other elements finishing the task. A few windows were intact; others gaped blackly and blankly. And all about was an air of mouldering decay, a sad echo of former splendour and graciousness.

She found her voice. "You knew this was here?"

"I knew there had been a house. I didn't know what remained." His voice was cool and impersonal, a hard stranger answering questions because he wasn't rude enough to ignore her completely. That was the way it would be.

"Do you know whose it was?" She took her eyes away from the fascinating relic of some bygone age to look at him. He nodded, their eyes meeting briefly, and his were cold.

"Yes. An eccentric, name of Joseph Cumberland, lived here in the house for over thirty years until his death about five years ago."

"Not alone?" Faint horror coloured her words.

"No – but nearly. He had two or three manservants. No women. He was a woman-hater," and his voice was quite expressionless when he said that. "He was a near-millionaire. It's rumoured that he expressed the desire in his will that the island – this island – should be left to the next man to land on it. As far as I know, nobody has ever been here since he died," and he strode away towards the gaping front door before the full impact of his words had sunk into Isla's still stunned brain.

Then they did, and she took a deep breath. Had he told her like that, in that casual, throwaway manner, deliberately? It would seem so, for there had been a note of almost grim amusement in his words. If the rumour were true – and why not if the man had been eccentric? – it would seem that Kyle, as a result of a storm, had become the possessor of an island. How ironic. And the words flashed into her mind the next moment: Kyle's Kingdom. It was almost funny – and yet not. For how bad were his motives – how very bad the reason why they had to be here in the first place. Swallowing hard, Isla went after him to where he stood just at the doorway looking at the hallway which had sunlight slanting in on it.

He put out his arm as if to stop her going any further. "Wait," he ordered. "The floorboards are rotten. Don't go in." She could see furniture still remaining in the hall, a table and an upright chair, and a mat on the floor that had almost been eaten away, and was of a colour that blended in with the wood. She looked at the rug, or what remained of it, and could see traces of a pattern, so badly weathered as to be almost invisible. Somehow it crystallised all Isla's feelings about the place. There was a sad

75

atmosphere clinging almost visibly to the very walls before them. She didn't like it. She turned away and said: "I'll wait here," and went down the verandah steps. Now, looking at from where they had come, she could see why the house had been built just where it had. In front of them, the trees from which they had so recently emerged, but to the right was a lake sparkling in the sun, sheltered partly by rich flowering shrubs and trees. Hibiscus flowers grew in profusion, soft pinks and mauves open to the warmth, delicate flowers she had only seen carefully nurtured in plant pots now growing in wild and beautiful disorder.

Isla walked towards the lake, and in the trees surrounding it she could now see another rare exotic flower. Orchids twined themselves sensuously round the trunks. She stopped, overwhelmed by the beauty, and looked round her, then at the lake. The shimmering sun had hidden all but the glittering surface before. Now, standing directly before it, she could see that it was not a natural basin but a tiled swimming pool. Blue tiles gleamed faintly below the surface, many cracked now with neglect, but the whole giving a gracious pleasant effect. A natural spring gushed in at one end – which made it appear that the pool's water was constantly changed. She knelt down and ran her fingers through the water. It stirred slightly, causing ripples, and a brightly coloured bird darted down from a tree, skimmed across the surface and vanished as silently as it had come. Something moved only feet away from her and Isla looked at the tiny green lizard panting in the heat. She knew if she moved too abruptly, the small creature would vanish nearly as fast as the bird.

The air was still and heavy, filled with rich, almost dizzying perfumes of the flowers which surrounded her. For a moment she forgot why she was there; Kyle had vanished – she neither knew nor cared where – and here, away from the house, there was a different atmosphere, a restful sense of peace and calm. Perhaps the eccentric recluse hadn't been so strange after all. Any man who could build his house so near to this natural beauty, and make a pool that appeared as if it belonged just there, could not have been entirely unfeeling – even if he was a misogynist, Isla smiled faintly to herself. What better person could he have left the place to? For if Kyle were not a hater of women how could he have taken such a job as he had? She stood up suddenly. Questions like that were better not asked – even mentally. They were too disturbing. Her whole body was damp with heat and exertion, and the pool was tempting, but Isla resisted. They were here to look for food.

She could imagine the expression on Kyle's face if he returned and saw her swimming in the pool: that blank shuttered look, the quiet patience that wasn't really – it was just an act. And Isla didn't want to see that, so she waited where she was until he came round from the back of the house.

"I've had a good look round," he said, coming towards her through the thick long grass that had once been a well cared for lawn. "And there's a great deal of wood we can get out of there – either from the body of the house itself or the remains of the furniture. We'll have it stacked ready somewhere to be lighted if there's the slightest trace of a plane in the sky or a ship on the horizon."

That seemed sensible. She nodded. "Of course. On the beach, you mean?"

"No. The highest point of the island." He pointed behind the house. "I've just been round the back. You can't see it from here, but there's a rise in the ground a few hundred yards along, and a fairly flat rocky plateau. That will do fine. We'll get old wood and greener younger wood – that will make plenty of smoke – which is precisely what we need."

Perhaps he'd been stranded on a desert island before, she thought wryly. He seemed to be cool enough about everything, shrewdly assessing their needs and planning how to cope. Perhaps too he made a habit of restoring runaway daughters to their wealthy fathers – which would explain the ease with which he had wooed her and persuaded her to go away for a few days with him when he was still a comparative stranger.

"No wonder you can afford a plane," she said softly, hardly aware that she had spoken aloud until he asked:

"What did you say?"

She looked quickly, guiltily, at him. "Nothing – I was thinking aloud." But when she saw his face, she wondered if he had heard the words – and if he wondered why she should have said them.

If he had, he was not going to take her up on it. "We'll get enough food to last us for today," he went on, and some of Isla's tension left her. The thought of another fight left her weak. "Then we can attend to the bonfire –" a deliberate pause, "I mean, I can – unless you want to help."

"Yes, I do. There's not much else to do, is there?" she

asked. "And I'm stronger than I look."

"I don't doubt it." They were moving away from the lovely pool while they spoke, and Isla took a last quick glance behind her. She would be back again, she knew, and in a small way it was something to look forward to. Such a peaceful place, and an atmosphere of calm that she found hard to describe.

And a minute later she knew another, possibly more important reason why the recluse had built his house just where he had. No sooner were they in the other belt of trees behind the pool than Isla saw the most enormous bunches of bananas growing on trees. She stopped in amazement, then went forward slowly and touched the nearest hand of tiny very yellow bananas with questing fingers.

She heard Kyle laugh. "Honey bananas. They're very sweet – much sweeter than the others. Here," he broke off a few and handed her two, "try those – you'll know why they're called honey bananas when you do."

She peeled and bit into the firm creaminess. It was a very pleasant sensation, and yes, there was that faint elusive taste mingling with banana that could have been honey. She forgot her enmity. "Gorgeous!" she exclaimed, then, remembering, sobered.

"Yes. Aren't they just?" He was cool enough for them both, she thought.

In the following hour they found a veritable treasure trove of food of all kinds, both fruit and vegetables. Loaded up, they made their way down to the beach, arriving there much further along, well past both airstrip and plane so that they had to walk back.

Isla found that she was tired. It was only partly due to the heat. Emotions of varying kinds had drained her too, so that after they had eaten she was scarcely able to keep her eyes open. It was so hot, too hot to do much except rest. Perhaps Kyle sensed her state, for he said, as they cleared away the fish bones, and skin from the bananas:

"I'm going to have a siesta. I suggest you do too."

"Yes, I will."

"It's too hot in the hut – the plane's not safe – and if you lie down in the trees you could get eaten by ants or worse." She looked at him in alarm. Was there the faintest trace of amusement on that tanned handsome face? Difficult to tell.

She kept calm. "What do you suggest? Where are *you* going?"

He shrugged. "I've been giving it some thought. There are two inflatable life rafts in the hold. One each," this with the slightest emphasis that might or might not have meant anything. "I'll get those out. They should be safe enough."

And he strode off towards the plane. Isla waited. He brought back not only the two life rafts, which resembled well packed orange-coloured paddling pools in their deflated state, but also a packet wrapped in thick polythene. He handed this to her.

"There are three flares in there," he told her. "If – when – we see a plane or boat, we'll send one up – as well as getting the bonfire going." She held the packet and turned it over curiously. Inside were three sticks of dynamite – or so it seemed.

"These?" she asked. "You mean the things that go up

like a rocket?"

"Yes. And I'll show you how to use one. If I have to sprint away to get the fire going you'll be doing the sending off."

"I see." A pang of dismay struck her. She must listen to his instructions carefully. There must be no mistakes in such a vital matter when every second would count.

He said softly: "They're not difficult," as if he understood.

The life rafts were self-inflating – and done in a matter of seconds. They swelled and grew with a whoosh and whistle that was faintly unnerving to Isla in her tense state. Then she looked at them in dismay. Kyle's voice caught her mood.

"You'll soon get used to it," he said, as if amused.

"I'm sure I will – and as you say, they'll be so much better than sleeping on the ground and being eaten by ants," she answered.

He began to drag one towards the trees, and under the first patch of shade, he stopped. "There you are," he said. "Get a blanket from the hut if you need one to lie on. I'm away to the house, but I won't be long." She didn't ask him why. She didn't care. She was just thankful that he wasn't going to stay. With any luck, she thought, I'll be asleep before he comes back. And so she was.

When Isla woke up the air was slightly cooler, and for a moment she did not know where she was. A pattern of greenery traced in sharp outline above her head moved in gentle sympathy with the slightest of breezes and she watched for a few minutes before sitting up and looking out towards the sea. White horses on the surface of the water told that the breeze was much stronger away from the sheltering trees, and she watched the foamy breakers rushing in to die on the sand. The other life raft was several yards away, but of Kyle there was no sign. And no sound. Perhaps some miracle had happened; perhaps he had found a way off the island, and left her alone. Only a second, the feeling, but she knew instant sharp dismay and shook her head, as if to make it go away. That would be the worst punishment of all, to be left alone there. What a ridiculous thought to have! That was one thing he would never do. She was worth too much money to him – and at *that* thought Isla scrambled out of the life raft and stretched herself. She had no idea of the time, her watch was in the Nissen hut with her clothes, and suitcase. And she wasn't going to call him. Let him stay away as long as he chose.

She gathered her bone-dry clothes from the bushes and went into the hut to change. The heat retained from a day of sunshine made it like an oven, and she dressed quickly, in a hurry to get outside to the cooler air from the sea.

Something dark moved and stirred as she bent to put on her sandals and she caught her breath at the sight of the huge fat spider on the bench. She moved away, running her tongue over her suddenly dry lips. She had an unreasonable fear of spiders, had had since childhood, and nothing would induce her to go near the bench – yet she needed her sandals. There might be more spiders on the floor.

"Oh!" She wrenched open the door and stepped out

quickly on to the safe, soft white sand. And Kyle, approaching, said:

"I thought I'd told you never to walk about without sandals?"

She looked blankly at him, dismayed. She should have been glad to see him. She could have answered: "Yes, I know, but I can't get them because there's a big spider in there and I was terrified of it." She could have done, but she had no intention of admitting anything like that to him. The fear made her voice sharp.

"Well, I decided to leave them off!" She tried to look casual, but only half succeeded, for the defiance was assumed.

"Then get them on," he said softly, and as if to emphasise it properly: "Now."

She moved away from the hut. With any luck the huge spider would have gone by the time she plucked up courage to enter again. If only *he* would leave her alone.

For the first time he looked puzzled, as if not understanding her attitude. The look vanished almost instantly, to be replaced by another, one she recognised. That arrogant, infuriating calm of his. "I see," he said. "You're in one of those moods, are you? Acting like the spoilt kid you are."

"If you like." She shrugged. Just as long as he didn't guess the real reason – she didn't care. She looked up at him, and smiled slowly. "If you want me to put them on, go and get them for me – they're in the hut."

His eyes narrowed, his mouth tightened. "You may be used to servants," he commented softly, "but you've picked the wrong man here. I don't wait on anybody. You get them yourself."

"No, I won't. Not until I'm ready." And they faced each other on the baking sand, and it was hot and dry to the soles of her feet.

"You'll get them now." He took her by surprise. She had noticed before the speed at which he could move if he chose. The next second she was twisted round and about to be propelled through the door, held by a pair of extremely powerful arms.

Isla screamed. Sheer blind terror filled her. She could no more have stopped that scream emerging than she could have stopped breathing.

"My God!" He jerked her back again and stared down at her. "You want damn well spanking for that!"

She couldn't speak, she could scarcely breathe for the panic that nearly choked her. Everything spun dizzily round, trees, sky, sand and sea in a dark whirling kaleidoscope of deadly fear.

"No!" she burst out at last. "No, please – I c-can't go in –" She had to stop to catch her breath. "The spider –" She was shaking now, trembling because she had nearly been taken in *there*. . . .

"What?"

It was no use. If she didn't tell him he would simply push her inside – and maybe leave her inside until she picked up the sandals. That thought was too unbearable.

"There's a s-spider on the bench. I saw it as I was about to put m-my sandals on. I couldn't – I couldn't –" She stopped and shook her head helplessly, unable to continue.

"And you're frightened of them?"

"Yes." There, it was said now, admitted at last. She waited for his burst of laughter.

He still had the capacity to surprise her. "Why didn't you just say so instead of making that scene?" he asked.

She looked up at him, and he took his hands away from her arms as if remembering where they were. "Because I thought you'd laugh at me," she said quietly.

He ran his fingers through his hair. "And I didn't, did I?"

She shook her head. "No."

"Listen," he said, "I thought you were being damned obstinate just then. And when you screamed –" he stopped, and the ensuing silence was eloquent. He took a deep breath. "You only needed to say. There's nothing wrong in being afraid of the sort of spiders you can get here. I'll go in. Where was it? On the bench, you said?"

"Yes. Just by my case. I panicked. I'm – I'm sorry."

He opened the door, and Isla instinctively took a step away. If he noticed he gave no sign, and a few seconds later he came out with her sandals. "Put them on," he told her.

She obeyed and asked: "Is it – still there?"

"No." He looked down and kicked at a pebble, as if it might be hiding underneath. "It could be anywhere. Don't worry, it's more frightened of us than we are of it."

That was easy for him to say. He didn't look as if he gave a damn about anything, she thought, as she watched him. "Do you want something else from there?" he went on.

"Not at the moment." But sooner or later she would

have to go in, and what then? They had left the food inside the hut, and already she was feeling hunger pangs. His sympathy – or at least the faint appearance of it – would soon vanish if Isla refused to go in for anything.

She said recklessly, not even understanding herself, "Don't worry, I've got over it n-now. I'll be careful when I need anything there, that's all."

"You're not a very good liar," he said quietly.

"What do you mean?"

"You know damn well. You're terrified –" he put up his hand as she would have tried to deny it. "For heaven's sake don't argue, woman. I'm not going to bite your head off for being scared of spiders. In any case, if it was a tarantula, you'd have good reason. It's not likely you'd get bitten, and as you're young and healthy, it's not likely you'd die if you were, but in the circumstances we're not going to take silly risks. Now, when you want anything from the hut, you tell me. Okay?"

The relief was overwhelming. "Yes," she said, and managed a smile.

"All right. I'll go in and get the food. We'll eat in the shade over there," he pointed, "then we'll decide where we're going to sleep tonight." He went in, leaving Isla to stand outside. He had only been gone a few moments when she heard an exclamation, and her heart leapt in alarm. Before she could move, or call out, Kyle appeared in the doorway, his hands clasped together as if he held something in them. . . . And she knew. "Oh no –" she shook her head from side to side. "Oh –"

"Hold on. I just want you to *look*. Stay where you are. I swear I won't let it near you." And he lifted the top hand away to reveal an ugly, hairy black spider in the centre of his palm. The cold sweat of fear broke out on Isla's body.

"Just tell me if that's what you saw."

"I – I – think so." It was difficult to speak, her mouth was so dry.

"Are you sure?"

"Yes, it was that one, I'm sure. W-why?"

"Good." He turned away and dropped the spider on a leafy green shrub, where it instantly scuttled away to vanish. "Because that was harmless – or I wouldn't have wasted time picking it up, I can assure you. And if that was the one you saw there's really nothing to worry about. Tarantulas are very unlikely here. I wanted to be sure, that's why I brought it out for you to see. Not to scare you."

The spider had gone now, but the crawling sensation persisted, all along Isla's spine. To think he had actually *touched* it – picked it up in his hands and carried it out to her. She looked at him. "You didn't kill it," she said, and it seemed an odd thing to say, but she couldn't think of anything else at that moment, so blank was her mind at the memory.

"No. I don't believe in killing anything unnecessarily. It's not done me any harm – nor you. And would killing it have made you any less afraid?"

"No," she shook her head. She felt she had to make something clear to him. "I didn't mean it quite like that. I didn't *want* you to kill it – but I assumed you would."

His mouth twisted slightly. "Did you? I wonder why?" he said quietly.

Isla turned away. The conversation was taking a turn she felt unable to cope with. There was something about this man she could not understand. There was this strength about him that made her feel helpless, and this, combined with what she had discovered about him made him a powerfully disturbing personality. "Weren't you going to get the food?" she asked, keeping her eyes towards the crippled plane. "I'm hungry."

"Yes, of course." He went inside the hut and the tension that had built up was dispersed. But the second that he had gone she looked towards the bush where he had put the spider. That had gone, but how many more were there?

It was dark by the time they had finished eating. Coffee bubbled in a pan on the fire on the sand, and Isla sat watching the red glow of burning twigs, and smelling the delicious aroma of good Brazilian coffee mingling with the smoke.

Stars appeared and became brighter as the sky rapidly changed from near white to purple velvet. How suddenly the night came in this part of the world, and how different from anything she had ever known was this place. Kyle leaned over and removed the pan and carefully filled their two beakers. Powdered milk was definitely a poor substitute for fresh, and they had agreed to ration it to this one cup a day, drinking the others black. How odd, she thought, as she watched him carefully measure a spoonful of the white powder into each cup, how much can you look forward to something that normally you would loathe. There was a sharp click as the lid snapped back into place and he put the tin down beside him.

"Thank you." She took the proffered beaker, and sipped the hot coffee slowly. They observed a truce at mealtimes – unspoken but in its own way explicit. And now there was only the glow from the embers giving them any light at all. Kyle spoke suddenly.

"I said I'd show you how to light the flares, didn't I?"

"Yes. Are you going to do it now?"

"No. In the morning. I want to be up at dawn and finish building the bonfire at the top."

"Did you – were you doing it this afternoon while I rested?" For some reason she felt guilty.

"Yes. I decided I didn't want a sleep after all." His tone was odd, slightly curt, unusually so for him.

"I'll come with you in the morning. I said I wanted to help."

"I know you did. I've not forgotten. Only sometimes I work better alone."

I'm sure you do, she thought. How nice to be so utterly capable. She stood up abruptly and picked up her coffee. "What time is dawn?" she asked.

"At this time of the year? About six. I'll wake you."

She finished her coffee, took the two dirty plates and his empty beaker together with her own and walked down to the water where she crouched to clean them with a never-failing mixture of salt water and sand.

Faint phosphorescence lit the water. It glowed softly nearby, and was strangely beautiful. What a romantic place! And if she were here with someone who really cared for her, how wonderful it could be. But with him – Isla's lips tightened. She must not think about it. Useless anger was an emotion that could make you ill, she knew. She turned to look back, and saw his dark outline as he crouched down putting more branches on the glowing red embers of the fire. The silhouette was sharply etched, a big powerful man who was afraid of nothing – not even, she remembered suddenly, spiders. Had anyone ever hurt *him* the way he had hurt her? she wondered. Impossible. He was all steel. How difficult it was becoming to think of the gentle, *caring* way he had behaved in Rio de Janeiro. And on Trintero too, the ride, the visit to George's – and the swim.

Isla paused in the act of picking up the plates from where they lay on the sand. There had been a special atmosphere during the swim – and afterwards on the beach, when he had taken her in his arms and kissed her. She felt herself go warm at the memories as they rushed back very vividly. And one thing was certain, she knew that now as well as she had when it had happened. He had not been unmoved then, during that brief passionate embrace. That had been no act. She saw again his face, the dark expression in his eyes that nothing could disguise. He had desired her then – and had suddenly found the control to push her away and say what he had. Isla picked the plates up slowly. An idea was forming – just a faint one, but for the moment it was enough. There was plenty of time to think about it later. She smiled to herself, a small secret smile that he couldn't see anyway because it was too dark. And as she walked towards him, and saw him waiting for her, the idea grew slightly, and she knew she was going to try it.

The fear of a spider creeping over her in the night was still with Isla when she crawled into the orange life raft to sleep a few hours later. Kyle was only feet away, and that was another disturbing factor. There was nothing to be done about it, she knew that, which was why she had deliberately tried to tire herself out by going for a long walk after their meal. She had set off along the beach with only the torch Kyle had given her, one he had taken from the plane. He had made no protest when she had told him what she intended, merely shrugged.

The beach was long, wider in some parts than others, the sand always smooth and soft underfoot, and the sea only feet away, deceptively quiet and beautiful, concealing the many dangers that lurked a distance out. It was very warm, the air still heavily scented with the many different varieties of flowers that grew in wild profusion all over the island. This part was new to Isla. She and Kyle had only been upwards, and in the opposite direction. She was unafraid. After the shattering events of the previous days, she wondered what could happen that might be worse. Spiders? There would hardly be any on the sand, but she kept her finger on the torch button, just in case. Nothing stirred. Occasional faint gleams from the bushes, little pinpricks of light that twinkled like miniature red stars, told of glow-worms, harmless insects that came to life in the darkness. Even the birds slept, and the only sound came from the sea, from far away, where unknown creatures lived their lives as they had done for millions of years. She looked out towards the water and wondered how long they would be trapped on this unnamed island with its decaying house and air of mystery.

Yes, that was it. Isla stood very still as she considered the thought. There was this certain disquieting atmosphere to the place, not caused solely by Kyle's and her relationship, it was more than that. There was a strange sensation of desolation and loneliness surrounding them, and she wondered at the man who had lived there for so many years. In spite of the beauty of the place, and all his money, she doubted that he had been happy. Perhaps his spirit lingered there, disapproving of a woman stepping at last on to these shores.

It was all speculation, of course. Isla moved slowly onwards. The plane, and Kyle, would have been completely out of sight even if it had still been daylight, for the beach curved gradually all the time, and she wondered how long it would take her to walk all the way round, or even if it were possible. Kyle had not said how large the island was. Perhaps he didn't know himself – or care. Perhaps he didn't care about anything at all. Isla's fingers tightened on the torch. She would see. She would soon know.

CHAPTER SIX

IT wasn't going to be too obvious, Isla had already decided that. Subtlety was the keyword. She had woken early the next morning, before Kyle, and crept quietly towards the hut. It wasn't until she was inside that she remembered about the spider.

She took a deep breath. Damn spiders! This was more important than her fear. She searched her case and found what she was looking for, a crisp cotton sundress in deep blue, carefully folded at the bottom. She had brought it on the supposed holiday, intending to wear it on Trintero, but had forgotten. Now she was glad that she had. She knew she looked fabulous in it, had in fact bought it in Rio since meeting Kyle, but had never had the chance to wear it. Simply cut, terrifically expensive, it was low-necked, with two thin shoulder straps, a full short skirt at the front of which was one large pocket with a flower on. She laid it out, found her comb, and her lipstick which had nearly melted in the intense heat, and set them beside the dress.

Then she ran out to the sea, kicked off her sandals, and went for a quick refreshing swim. Kyle was lighting the fire when she came out of the sea. She greeted him:

"Good morning," and gave a sunny smile.

For a brief moment she could see he was startled, then he answered her:

"Good morning, Isla. I'm going to try and catch a fish

for breakfast – but first I need a shave. I won't be long."

"There's no hurry." And she vanished into the hut. It had been easier to take the first step than she had imagined. Seeing him like that had taken her by surprise. She had expected him to still be sleeping. She dressed, smoothing the crisp blue material over her waist, and tried a quick pirouette. Then she combed the rebellious curls, still damp, into order, put on a light coat of lipstick – and remembered her perfume, still in her handbag. It was a tiny bottle of "Jolie Madame," one of her particular favourites, and she smoothed some behind her ears and at the pulse on her throat and wrists. This was it. The campaign was about to start. Her heart beat faster, and she smiled to herself as she stepped outside into the melting sunshine.

He had propped a mirror in a cleft stick and was concentrating on removing the lather from his face with quick strokes of the razor. Too engrossed to look up at her at first – and then he did, and the razor faltered – just for a second – but she heard his muttered: "Damn," and saw red mingling with the white as he picked up a cloth and wiped his cheek.

Isla stood very still, not daring to smile now. The dress had had more effect than she had intended, it seemed. The moment passed, he finished his task and stood up and strode away to the plane without another word.

"Oh dear, did you cut yourself?" she enquired when he returned. The piece of paper that was sticking to his cheek told its own story, but he looked at her, equanimity regained.

"It looks like it," he answered shortly.

Isla let her eyes widen slowly. "It won't stop you catching a fish for breakfast, will it?" she enquired sweetly. "I mean – aren't sharks supposed to go for blood?"

For a moment she wondered if she had gone too far, then he gave a twisted smile. "We can always catch one, can't we?" he answered. "It would last us longer – though without a fridge it would get rather high after a few hours." His eyes were on her, expressionless now, no telling what he was thinking. But she had seen enough, in just those few seconds, to tell her what she wanted to know. Not quite as invulnerable as he would like her to believe he was. And that thought gave her a quiet inner confidence.

She went to fetch the beakers and coffee and set them out on the sand near the fire, and Kyle took the pan and filled it with water from their store in the shade behind the Nissen hut. "You want coffee first?" he asked her, putting the pan on the fire.

"Please. It's so hot, isn't it? And then, when we've eaten, we can go up and collect that wood." Then she remembered. "And you're going to show me how to light the flares, aren't you?"

"Straight after coffee. Do you want a cigarette?"

"Not if you're short. I can take them or leave them."

"I've got a packet. When they're gone, that's it. It doesn't bother me."

He lit two with a glowing twig from the fire while she made the black coffee, and handed her one. Their hands touched briefly as he did so, a small electric shock that she wondered if he had noticed too. He sat back on the dry sand, looking out to sea as he smoked the cigarette, and Isla watched him. His profile was etched sharply against the background of pale clear sky, a strong outline, his features composed, that determined chin, jutting at an angle that could, she felt sure, be arrogant. And she wondered quite suddenly what was going on in his mind. Of what was he thinking as he sat there drinking his coffee? Difficult to tell, as it always was. She had not known, for instance, of his planning to take her back to England. How clever he had been, how very clever. And if I have anything to do with it, she thought, you'll come to regret the day you decided to do that. And her hand tightened on the handle of the beaker, and Kyle looked at her at that precise moment, almost as if her thoughts had reached him.

"I'll go and fetch the flares," he said, his eyes narrowing slightly.

"Of course. I'm waiting to learn," she said – and smiled. He stood up, tipped the dregs of his coffee into the sand and walked away. When he had gone, Isla stood up herself and smoothed particles of sand from her skirt. She walked slowly down to the sea to wash the beakers out, not in a hurry, let him wait for her. She was careful not to splash salt water on to her dress as she rinsed out the beakers, and without looking round, knew that Kyle was standing by the fire. Then, when every trace of coffee was removed at last, she strolled back.

He opened the packet and took one of the sticks out, and handed it to Isla. "Don't actually touch the top," he warned her, "but you see that bit –" he was standing very close to her now, of necessity, to instruct her, and she knew that he would be well aware of her perfume.

"Yes, I see it," and she lifted her face up to look at him. She was just in front of him, and her hair brushed his cheek as she turned, she knew that. She heard him take a deep breath. A small secret triumph filled her. She was certain now. She listened to what he was saying with only half her mind. The other half was busily plotting ahead. Then, as she handed the flare back to him, she said: "Tell me again," and kept her hand on his for a moment. "Show me now."

He took her hand in his and showed her what she had to do to ignite the flare, and it was warm on hers and strangely disturbing so that she could not look up at him, lest he should see. His long fingers were supple and strong – gentle too – then he moved abruptly away, and the spell was broken.

"That's it," he said. "You've got the hang of it now. I'll put them back just inside the hut, on the bench," and he strode away, leaving Isla standing where he left her. She rubbed her fingertips tentatively together where his had touched, and the tingle remained. He came out a minute later in his swimming trunks, carrying a knife, shouted: "I'm going for a fish," and ran down to the sea. Isla watched him go, for it would have been difficult not to. He moved swiftly and silently, an athlete in perfect condition, a superb swimmer too. Economical of movement, once in the water he swam quickly out – and suddenly vanished. She found she was holding her breath. It was ridiculous, of course, he was not far enough out to be in any danger, but – who could know what lurked in those depths? He had a knife, he was strong and sure, but a kind of tension filled Isla. For all her dislike, she wanted

97

no harm to come to him. . . . And then his head reappeared, and she let out her breath in a deep sigh. It was all right. She watched as he came nearer and when at last he was wading out, she walked towards him, not knowing why. He carried a fish, a fat white shiny fish that gleamed in the sun.

"Build the fire up, will you, Isla, while I fillet this?" Already the gulls were gathering overhead in anticipation, swooping and gliding in the warm air, prepared to wait patiently for any titbits that might come their way. Isla did as she was bid and watched Kyle skilfully cut and bone the fish, tossing the waste parts away to be grabbed by the greedy birds almost before they landed. They cooked the fish in a flat pan taken from the galley, and ate it with honey bananas. An unusual combination, thought Isla almost with amusement, but quite delicious – and that was all that mattered.

Half an hour later they were making their way up towards the house that had once belonged to Joseph Cumberland. Too hot to work, yet it had to be done, and soon, for to lose the opportunity of escape, if a plane flew near enough, or a boat was seen, was unthinkable. How long had they been there? Isla had to think, for time seemed to blur into a golden haze in this warm, lazy place. Two nights, two whole nights, and a day just begun, and in that time nothing. Not a single sound that could be a plane engine, nor a faint smudge on the horizon. And how much longer would it be then, before they were found? A vision of days stretching endlessly ahead, on and on, suddenly came to Isla, and she stopped in her tracks. Oh no!

"What is it?" Kyle had halted too, and was turning

round, not impatient, merely enquiring.

She didn't want to tell him. "Nothing. I just had to catch my breath," she lied, and then, because of this new resolve that nothing would alter, she smiled. She didn't stop to consider that she might be playing with fire. That thought never even entered Isla's head.

It was only an hour or so later that the storm began – quite suddenly, as storms do, and it took them by surprise. They had been busily piling up wood from the house. Kyle, still in his swimming trunks, dripped with sweat as he lifted and moved and ripped the heavy planks of wood from their places. Isla carried the smaller ones to where he had heaped the first basic beginnings of their bonfire, and he followed with the larger ones.

She looked longingly at the swimming pool as she passed it on her way back each time. How wonderful to sink into that cool water and float, feeling the sun on your face! But she had offered to help, and she was going to do so. And she would keep on until he told her to stop – and just as the moment, that seemed never.

He was on his way to the bonfire, and Isla was using the moment's respite to take a breather, when the sky turned black, the heavens opened with a roar and a rush, and she was stunned by a vivid blue-yellow flash of fire that seemed to leap and echo deafeningly about her. And the huge outline of Kyle, running towards her, somehow completed the image of terror. She wanted to scream, but didn't. The next second she was being practically lifted into the house. There was one room where the ceiling was virtually intact. It was small, little more than a glorified broom cupboard off the kitchen, but for some reason it had remained relatively unscathed. The next moment they were inside, watching the dry wood soaking up the huge raindrops that plopped and pattered all around them.

Outside thunder rumbled, right overhead, terrifyingly near and loud, and the flashes of lightning came simultaneously, and Isla, remembering the other, fateful storm, was frightened. Kyle was beside her, and the plan mingled with her fear and she turned to him so that her left arm was against his chest, and the rain dripped down him, all the way from his hair and face, and she could still see the cut that had been, in a way, her fault, and she smiled very slightly.

"I'm frightened," she said, and began to shiver. The shiver was only partly of fear. There was something here, some indefinable tension, because the two of them were standing there in that tiny space surrounded by old cupboards and the smell of rain and the fainter traces of Isla's perfume still lingering. . . . And he was aware of it too, for he moved and stirred as if uneasy, although perhaps not knowing why.

"We're safe here," he said. "These storms soon pass. You'll see."

"Yes – but I keep thinking about the plane –" and she faltered. Then, as the most vivid, frightening flash of all came, and it seemed almost as if it leapt about the floor in the room outside, she clutched him in utter terror . . . and felt his arms go around her, around her shoulders, comfortingly.

"Stay still. Count twenty slowly to yourself," he said,

but she wasn't listening. The fear had been replaced by another emotion, a deep, disturbing one she scarcely understood herself, and her heartbeats were rapid and erratic, for his bare arms were very warm, nearly dry now, very strong, and they were holding her quite firmly. It was probably the best chance she would have. The storm might pass in a minute, she knew that. She began counting inwardly, waiting only for the next lightning flash. One – two – three – four – five. It came then, and she moaned and pressed herself closer to him as if overcome by terror, her arm at his back, touching his bare skin lightly, almost caressingly, as though in fear – but it wasn't fear that filled her now, it was a strange kind of excitement, for in another second he would kiss her. . . .

"Isla," he whispered, as he bent his head, and his voice was lost, for his mouth was against her hair – then moving her head, lifting her face to him as she said:

"Yes. Oh, when will this go away?" She was frightened he would feel her heartbeats, but then it didn't matter, for his mouth came down on hers in a kiss of startling, exciting suddenness. Lips that were warm and gentle, just like they had always been, but now it was different as Isla let herself respond. Difficult not to anyway, but inside her the small core of scheming that never left her, because he was going to be taught a lesson. And she was going to teach it to him. Soft responsive lips meeting his, and the air round them sizzled and crackled, but it wasn't due to the storm now as she melted her body against his, sensing his growing awareness and response –

"Good try, Isla." He took his mouth away, and his eyes were dark, but his voice was cool – very cool. "Boy, but you're a good one, aren't you?"

The words weren't right. They hit her like a blow and she jerked her head back, and he began to laugh, softly at first, then loudly, as if in release of tension.

"Wh-what do you mean—?" Eyes wide, she still trembled from the kiss.

"I just wanted to see how far you would go. Do you think I don't *know* what you're up to?" Scorn tinged the words, and she tried to move away, but now he held her and the grip was no longer pleasant. It was too firm for that.

"Let me go," she whispered fiercely.

"When I've finished. What were you intending to do? Reduce me to a grovelling wreck – or make me fall for you?" His voice was hard now, hard and cruel. "No chance, Isla. It would take more of a woman than you –"

She wrenched her arm free and raised it to hit him hard, but he was too swift for her. He caught and held her hand tightly to her side. A strange intense anger filled her, and she twisted violently to be free, for she didn't want to hear any more.

Her breast heaved in the effort to get away from this awful man. "I *hate* you!"

"I know you do. Which made your change of character so much more difficult to understand. God, what sort of fool do you think I am? It stuck out a mile, the perfume, lipstick, that dress –" he looked down in amusement at her. "No one in their right mind is going to wear a dress like that for heaving chunks of wood about!" He released her hand, and ran his fingers down the side of her face and neck, and as she flinched, added softly: "See what I mean? Now you cringe – my, what an effort it must have been for you to actually kiss me. How did you manage that?"

She wasn't going to speak to him. The feeling that filled her was too intense to allow her to answer the bitingly cruel words. She stood there not moving, waiting for him to set her free. He was too strong to fight physically. She just wanted to get away from him now, to cleanse herself of his touch, the touch that burned with its contempt. It was as if he realized. She saw his expression change fractionally; the next moment he no longer held her. Tension smouldered, needing only a spark to set it on fire. Kyle's face, his *hateful* face looking down at her, he standing easily, yet she knew he was as tense as a coiled spring, and just now, at this moment, entirely unpredictable. She backed away from him, towards the outer room, uncaring of the storm, wanting only to escape from him. He didn't speak, merely watched her, and his gaze was too steady and disconcerting for Isla.

She turned and ran out, out of the wreck of a house, down the path to the beach, anywhere to be away from him. Anywhere.

Breathless, rain-soaked, she reached the Nissen hut and went in, leaving the door wide open. Inside it was pleasant because the rain had cooled it, although in an hour it would be like an oven again because already the rain was drying, steaming away in the sunlight that had returned. The storm was over.

The rain had revived the plants and trees, cleansed the sand. The other storm had only just begun. Isla sat on the bench, her whole body aching with nervous tension, and leaned forward, putting her head wearily into her hands.

She wanted so much to cry, yet no tears would come.

So he knew, and her plan had failed, and the war was out in the open. She had no illusions about that. Kyle was a hard ruthless man who appeared to get exactly what he wanted. Isla looked up as a shadow darkened the doorway. Kyle stood there, looking at her. A prickle of fear ran down her spine. What would he do now? He stood there, a brooding giant of a man whose presence made her uneasy. She was no longer sure of anything. But one thing she knew. She must not let him see she was frightened. She stood up slowly, and it was a relief to have the bench behind her, for she wasn't quite sure how steady her legs would remain if she moved away from it. Her chin tilted defiantly, she said:

"What do you want?"

He came in slowly. "You!" was the disconcerting reply.

"Don't come any nearer." She looked swiftly round her.

"No bricks handy? Never mind, I'm not going to give you the good hiding you deserve – I don't hit women."

"Then get out. I don't want *you*."

"You're not staying here sulking all day. There's work to be done."

"I'm not doing any with you." She spoke flatly, without emotion.

"No?" He lifted one eyebrow. "You're going to be independent – look after yourself, you mean? Tell me, do you think you'll find it easy to catch a fish?"

"I'll live on fruit and vegetables."

"And drink water? That'll be nice for you. I can be twice as awkward as you can, and the sooner you realize that the better. You'll come off worst in any battle, I promise you." He stood there in front of her, a steely giant of a man who had suddenly become even more of a stranger than before.

"If that's how you want to play it – all right, go ahead. I'll manage." But even as she said it, her voice strong with reckless defiance, Isla had a quiver of dismay.

"Don't push me too far. You really are asking for it."

"Don't be so damned superior. Asking for what? Do you imagine that you're the only one who can survive on this place, just because you're a *man*? Don't make me laugh!"

She had begun now, and there was no chance of going back. "You're all the same. Women aren't helpless any more. I'm strong – I'll manage." It was a nightmare world, everything turning horribly wrong, and nothing, no way of getting out of it, that was what was so awful.

And Kyle Quentin looked hard at her, said: "If that's the way you want it, it suits me fine," and he walked out.

Isla put her hand to her face. That was it. No turning back now. In a strange way, she was on her own.

She went to the spring to wash her clothes soon afterwards. There was no sign of Kyle, either near the plane or in the sea, and she supposed that he had gone back to the house to finish building the bonfire. There was a vast empty silence all about her, even the distant roar of the sea muted, and the gulls had gone. They would return later when he caught a fish for his meal. His, not theirs.

105

For she knew with dread certainty that he would not weaken in any way. She laid the clothes out to dry on the bushes and took her blue silk headscarf to gather fruit and vegetables in. Suppose he refused to let her use the pan for cooking? Or the fire? It was clear that he didn't intend to share his coffee, so the others were feasible. Isla, struggling upwards in dazzling sunshine towards the fruit grove, had a pain in her side, almost like a stitch, but she didn't stop walking. She had no idea of the time, but the sun was still high, and she wasn't a bit hungry, only thirsty, very thirsty. So when she returned, she would seek out fuel for a fire of her own. Then she would creep into the plane and find another pan, anything to heat water in. He might not give her one, but surely he wouldn't take one from her if she already had it? She wasn't even sure of that any more.

She felt dizzy from the heat, and perspiration ran down into her eyes and blinded her so that she stumbled over a stone and nearly fell. She wiped her eyes and went on, and she would remember to pick several oranges this time. The juice would be a pleasant alternative to plain water.

She was busy for quite a while, choosing the ripest bananas and mangoes, several oranges, a few of the weird-looking things that tasted like potatoes. She put all thoughts of fish firmly out of her mind. She looked doubtfully at the small green limes and eventually picked two. She had enough now. Slowly she began to walk back down to the beach.

Kyle was emerging from the sea. Holding a fish – of course. His small fire glowed brightly, and the pan was beside it on the sand, waiting. Isla looked quickly away. She wasn't hungry anyway, the fruit would be sufficient for now. So she told herself, and was really beginning to believe it. When the most delicious aroma of cooking fish drifted across the still air to where she sat in the shade by the hut. She peeled an orange and bit into it, carefully saving the peel to use on the fire. The orange was delicious too, it really was, *quite* delicious, she told herself firmly.

There were magazines on the plane, and she had seen a paperback or two as well on board, in one of the sliding cupboards. She had to wait for a while until he had finished cooking and eating the fish, and then cleared away. Faint hunger pangs assailed her now, and before too long it would be dark, for night fell early and suddenly, she knew only too well. Why didn't he go for a walk or something? She glanced very casually across, but he seemed quite oblivious to her presence. She jumped up irritably and went to look for more branches and twigs. If it came to the worst, she would try and read by the flames.

He seemed to be taking his time. And then he was moving, getting up, going down to the water to clean his plate and the pan. She watched him, loathing him with a frustrated helpless anger that would not leave her. Then he was walking away, back towards the house. She waited, her heart leaping in sudden relief. She would give him a minute, then go to the plane. She counted carefully up to sixty, and it seemed to take an age. Silence. Even the faint crackling of branches had faded now. Isla got to her feet and walked very casually across to the plane, just in case. . . .

107

It was difficult to climb in, it was at such an angle, but she managed, and clambered across to lift out the books and magazines and leave them by the door. Then into the galley, very slowly, fearful of his return, as fast as she could, but it was difficult, it was almost like crawling along.

There were two more pans. She took the smaller one, and as she lifted it out, saw the tin of stewed steak at the side – a small tin, just enough for a meal for one person. Isla moistened her lips with her tongue, and the temptation was overwhelming.

She took it out and looked at it. It had a zipper top – simple to pull and remove – and bury afterwards. And just at that moment it seemed as if it would be the most delicious food in the world. She put it in the pan and made her careful way to the door. Five minutes later she was heating the meat in her pan on Kyle's fire. She didn't care any more. Even if he came back right now, it wouldn't make any difference. She was going to eat a beautiful meal of steak and gravy. She didn't even bother to put it out on the plate, she ate it out of the pan.

Isla had never enjoyed anything quite so much for ages. She looked at the empty pan when it was all gone, and wiped her finger gently round it. "Beautiful," she murmured. There was no time to waste just sitting there contemplating the superb repast. The tin had to be buried, the pan washed and hidden, the books put in her case, and her own fire lit. She stood up and took the tin behind the Nissen hut and dug with her fingers in the warm dry sand until the evidence was fully lost. She felt much better than she had done an hour previously. Almost uncaring of Kyle Quentin and his brutal treatment. Almost.

She had hidden all the papers in her case, taking out only one magazine, a weekly, full of articles and short stories and jokes. Her little fire burned brightly, the twigs crackling with yellow flame, sending tiny red sparks upwards to vanish into darkness. It had gone cooler with the going down of the sun, and the warmth was welcome. Isla lay on her stomach beside the fire and held the paper at such an angle that she could see the print.

From where she was she could also observe Kyle without him knowing. He had the torch on and was sitting crosslegged by his fire doing something that looked complicated with some tiny wires and pieces of metal. She wasn't sure if they were radio parts, or something from the house, and could not ask. That was what he was waiting for – for Isla to weaken, to admit that she could not manage on her own, and hated the loneliness of not speaking.

"I won't give in, I won't," she whispered fiercely to herself. She looked down to her magazine again, halfway through a short article on slimming that was almost funny under the circumstances, advising as it did that would-be slimmers should try a little grilled fish for Monday's lunch. Isla tried to smile at the unconscious humour of it all, and the words blurred and danced before her eyes. She blinked, blaming her inability to see the words on the dim light, but she knew, even before a large tear splashed on to the paper, that it wasn't the light at all. A sense of the most utter desolation filled her entire being. There seemed at that moment no sense at all to life, no more sense in struggling against a cruel fate that had landed her on an abandoned island with a man who had seemed to be everything she had ever wanted, a man with whom she had found herself beginning to fall in love – until his words. The most shatteringly cruel words anyone could have ever said to her – until the storm. He had excelled himself then. Nothing he had told her before could surpass his brutality and contempt after he had kissed her, stripping her last remnants of her pride with his taunts. One sentence stood out clearly; she would never forget it: "It would take more of a woman than you." That said it all. Isla put her head down on her arms. Quietly, she wept.

CHAPTER SEVEN

SLEEP was fitful that night. When Isla awoke the next
morning she felt tired and drawn. It was still early, and
dark, and as she sat up to rub her eyes, a faint thin strip
of red smudged the inky black horizon, sudden orange
flared in the sky, joyous and radiant, and the sun rose. Despite everything, she caught her breath at the sheer beauty
of it, and watched everything become lighter, filled with
rich gold instead of grey. There were no clouds in the sky,
and warmth touched her even as she climbed out of the
life raft and went slowly towards the hut to dress, today
in a pair of bright blue shorts and white sleeveless blouse.
Isla was deeply tanned now, to a rich gold, her dark curls
faintly bleached by the sun. She hadn't looked in a mirror
for days, and now there was no point. She didn't care
how she looked. She didn't know that she was more beautiful than ever before, even the faint shadows of fatigue
beneath her eyes only serving to enhance the utter femi-
ninity of her features.

Slim, long-legged, she ran down to the sea to splash
her hands and face in an effort to refresh herself. She
intended to eat fruit for breakfast, and then, later on,
as soon as the opportunity arose, take a tin of something
from the galley. And she had an answer prepared in case
Kyle caught her, an answer that might in some way help to
erase the sheer hurt of his cruel taunt to her the previous
day. There was plenty of time. He would be away soon,

111

up to the house, or to the grove for fruit and vegetables. Isla was learning to be patient.

She didn't speak when she saw him waken, she turned her back on him and walked to the hut for her breakfast. Even at the smell of coffee she didn't show the slightest flicker of response. The sweet tang of a fresh orange managed to take away any longing for that. She saw him clamber into the plane, and had a brief moment of unease in case he had gone for a magazine and might challenge her. She didn't think about the missing tin of meat at all.

Isla finished the orange, carefully peeled a mango and bit into the succulent sweetness of it. He was gone for quite a while, and she wondered why, until she remembered what she had seen him doing the previous evening with metal and wire. Her heart skipped a beat. Could he be mending the radio? Was it possible?

She stood up, about to cross to the aircraft and ask, then remembered. No, she could not. Her head spun round for a moment, and she leaned against the hut to steady herself. The heat, of course, and tiredness, that was all it was. Later on she would have a rest. The dizziness passed, but it left something behind, a slight feeling of sickness, that persisted for quite a while afterwards, and was then forgotten.

The sun rose higher and higher in the metallic blue sky, bringing with it intense heat. Even a swim in the pool failed to cool her, and she went back down to the beach after noon, feeling restless and uneasy. She wasn't even hungry, and eventually, to quench her insatiable thirst, cut into one of the small ripe limes and sucked it. The tangy flavour shocked her palate and teased it, but it had the effect of making her drink and enjoy several cups of water from the ever-cool constant spring.

She had heard tapping from the plane for quite a while, and it persisted even after she lay down for a sleep in the shade in the middle of the afternoon. The faint noise even accompanied her into her dreams, and turned into distant drumbeats from the band on George's terrace, where she was dancing with Kyle to an exotic samba.

The dream was colourful and pleasant, and seemed to turn everything back again into the magic world she had shared with him for just a few precious days. . . .

Then she woke up, and the dream fled before the reality as she knew again where she was; the tapping had stopped, and the day was cooler, and Isla's head burned like fire. She stood up and walked away from the life raft. Kyle was jumping down from the plane. He looked at her briefly but said nothing, then he turned and went into the trees that hid the path to the house. Isla waited, to give him time to get well away, then she walked across towards the plane. It was late afternoon, she had eaten only an orange and a mango that day, and the faint sick feeling was returning. There were no fires lit, but she didn't care. She would simply try and find something that could be eaten cold.

She felt sure that there was a tin of corned beef in the cupboard. It took her longer to climb into the plane than she expected, mainly because it seemed to have tilted more away from her. Or was it just higher? Difficult to tell. The whole framework seemed to be shaking as she eventually found herself inside and she touched a seat curiously, wondering why it should be so. Was it going to tip right over? She didn't much care. The faint buzzing noise in her ears would have been annoying if she had let it bother her, but that too seemed unimportant beside the overwhelming urge to find that tin of corned beef.

There it was! She lifted it out of the cupboard and turned to go back, then nearly fell down, because her balance was badly affected by the plane which was now shaking violently, moving across and tilting in huge waves, almost like a ship being tossed on a wild sea. She wanted to cry for help, but the words stuck in her throat and she stumbled across to the door, frightened at what was happening. And Kyle's voice cut into her panic as he said: "I thought I'd catch you if I came back." She looked down at him. Didn't he know? Couldn't he see? He stood there outside the plane, the sun turning him to a bronzed Greek god, lithe and muscular, poised to trap her, and she jumped down to the ground, the tin clutched tightly in her hand. Then she realized why he hadn't seemed at all bothered at the plane's violent movement – it hadn't been the plane at all, it was Isla herself. She was frightened. What's happening to me? she thought. Kyle's face blurred as she glared defiantly up at him.

"You're not taking it off me," she blurted out. "I don't *care!*"

"I said we'd save the tinned stuff." His voice seemed far away. Was he doing it deliberately?

"Go to hell," she answered, and began to walk away. He caught her arm just lightly, but it was the action that triggered off Isla's pent-up anger. She swung round on him, lashing out violently with her other arm, and he caught that too, and held her helpless, and dark angry

114

points lit his eyes.

"I don't say things for fun," a deep thread of controlled temper ran through his voice. "If I'm not able to catch a fish for any reason, we'll have something to fall back on. We won't if you eat it all. Now why don't you be sensible and eat with me?"

Isla wrenched her arm free and threw the tin as far as she could into the bushes. Something was driving her to act as she was, something she didn't understand at all. "Then go and get *that* yourself," she said. Her head and eyes hurt terribly, and she just wanted to lie down, but she wouldn't let *him* know that. . . .

"You little *bitch*!" he grated. "You can go and find it yourself right now." And he pulled her towards the bushes. She fought and struggled, but it was no use. He was far too strong to resist. Far too strong. . . . Isla went limp as a frightening wave of dizziness swept over her, and everything swam round in a crazy arc.

She heard his voice, and it was very far away, almost unrecognisable, but now she was falling, falling, and the sands were rushing up to meet her and it was really quite astonishing just how far away they were, miles and miles, in fact. And it was all happening in slow motion, for she was sure she felt his arms going round her, picking her up, lifting her away from the sands, carrying her somewhere. . . .

The water was fresh and cold to her face, and someone was holding the cloth and dabbing her cheeks with it, very gently. Isla opened her eyes. She lay on a blanket, in the shade of huge palm trees, and Kyle was there, kneeling beside her, holding a towel in his hand.

For a moment Isla was frightened that she would not be able to move or speak. And everything seemed very shadowy, almost as if it were night. Kyle spoke before she could even attempt to. "Try and sip this," he said. His voice was quite impersonal, certainly no longer angry. He tilted up her head and touched her lips with a beaker. The liquid was bitter and she instinctively pulled a face even before that first taste.

"Drink it all. You've a fever. It will help to cool you down." He spoke as though to a child, and Isla obeyed, too weak not to. She began to shiver helplessly.

"I'm sorry," she said, not sure what she meant, whether it was for throwing the tin away, or being ill, for she knew instinctively that something was very wrong with her.

"It's all right," the words were almost soothing. "Don't worry about anything. I'm going to fetch you a drink now. Lie still. You'll be better very soon." He stood up, looked down at her for a brief moment, then turned and went away.

He made her drink a full beaker of orange juice and water, wiped her face and hands, and told her: "I'm going to move you to the life raft. I'll try and keep you steady. Are you ready?"

"I don't — I don't want you to catch anything," she managed to whisper eventually.

Kyle laughed. "Don't worry about me. You've been bitten by some insect, it'll take a day or so to work out of your system. Until it does, you do as you're told, okay?"

He lifted her easily and lightly, carried her to the

orange life raft and laid her down in it. Evening was fast approaching, and Isla wondered for how long she had been blacked out. It was difficult to think, in any case. Thought hurt, even the effort of wondering what time it might be was painful and confusing. She was alternately hot and cold, her skin sore when she reached up to brush a hair from her face. And she was completely helpless, that was the worst thing of all.

He had turned away, was bending down as if looking for something in the bushes nearby. Then he turned back to her.

"Do you think you can eat anything?" he asked.

"No. I'm not hungry."

He seemed as if about to say something, then apparently thought better of it. "All right. I'm going to try for a fish. I won't be long. Will you promise not to move?"

The smile hurt, but she had to try. "I couldn't if I wanted to," she said faintly.

"You will soon. Don't be frightened." Then he was gone. Isla drifted off into a strange half sleeping, half waking state in which she heard voices and music, all slightly out of key and oddly frightening. She thought she was going to die. Shadows mingled and blended and one grew larger, looming over her as Kyle's voice said:

"Try and sit up, Isla. See, I've put a little fish on a plate for you. Will you just take some in a spoon?"

"Please – please –" she put out a shaky hand and clasped his. "Kyle, I'm frightened." And tears fell down her cheeks, tears of weakness, fever, and tiredness. She didn't know why she should do it; it was the last thing she had ever intended in the world, but it happened. She

117

didn't see his expression change, didn't see that hard face become gentler – just for a few moments. She couldn't see anything for the scalding tears that coursed down her face and blinded her. A muscle tightened in the man's jaw, he reached out a hand as if to touch her hair, then stopped himself. Without another word he got up and walked away, leaving her alone.

Strange dreams followed. In all of them Isla was lost and frightened, and trying to run away. The awful thing was that she neither knew where she was running from, or where to. Everything was a horrifying jumble of nightmarish incident, seemingly without any end. When she saw huge spiders crawling up her legs, she screamed – she heard the echo of that sound even in the midst of her own delirium, and after that it seemed that someone was with her. Comforting arms held her, she didn't know whose, and a soothing voice told her not to be scared.

She awoke, and it was pitch black night, and she felt a blanket lightly over her limbs. For a moment, one brief second, the fever abated, and Isla felt the dark shape by her side, holding her, and she was no longer frightened, even though Kyle seemed to be fast asleep. Then she too fell into a deep dreamless sleep.

The morning came in, orange and yellow and glorious, and Isla was alone when she woke to see the sky ablaze with the newly risen sun. She felt terribly weak, vaguely aware of soothing hands on her face and head with cooling wet cloths, and a bitter taste of medicine in her mouth. A memory of something that had passed during the night and the previous evening, and although she still felt ill, she knew she wasn't going to die.

"Try and drink this." It was Kyle. He looked as though he had slept little, his face drawn and hard in the bright morning light.

The drink was cool and Isla was thirsty. It was fresh lime juice, sharp and sweet at the same time. Her hands shook so much that he held the beaker for her. "We won't be here much longer, Isla," he said, but she didn't understand the words, so she just looked at him.

"The radio. I managed to mend it." He spoke slowly, no expression to tell her if he was joking or not, although it would be cruel to joke about a thing like that.

"No," she whispered faintly. "No –"

"Yes. Someone is looking for us. I've lit the bonfire. That's why I must go and keep a look-out. You must stay here."

Was he going to leave her behind? The nightmares might come true. She looked at him, and saw how hard and cruel he really was. She wouldn't let it happen. It mustn't. She would see that he didn't do such an unutterably horrid thing. Pretend to agree, her confused mind told her, and she nodded. "Yes, I'll stay here," she whispered.

She waited for him to go, counted up to a hundred, then began the painful journey out of the life raft. In her mind was the idea that if she could make it to the plane, she would be safe. Because even in the middle of the fever and confusion was the hard core of sense that told her a plane would have to land, and the only place it could do so was the airstrip, and she was going to be there – waiting.

She could not stand up. Her legs buckled under her and she lay on the sand by the life raft completely helpless. She could see the plane in the distance, a sad broken thin victim of a storm, and it looked terribly far away. Heat shimmered in front of her eyes, turning the sand to rippling gold, the distant sea to silver that shivered as if made of ice. Ice!

How tempting was the water. It beckoned her and she wanted to run down to it and throw herself in and swim away. . . . There was sand in her mouth, a harsh gritty taste, and she pulled a face. Very carefuly she eased herself up, and began to crawl along towards the concrete airstrip. She had to stop because the effort was great, she had to stop and rest, and thought she would never make it, but desperation drove her to keep trying. He mustn't leave her behind, he must not. Nearer and nearer, every faltering movement of arm and leg taking her that bit closer to the baking hot concrete. In her mind she imagined she heard the distant drone of a plane, growing gradually louder and nearer. How strange she should dream of planes when she was so near to one! How very odd. She must go on now; perhaps it was Kyle's plane she could hear – perhaps he'd mended the engine as well as the radio. Why, it was quite funny. Isla began to laugh, and when she did that she couldn't move, so she lay down on the sand next to the baking hot airstrip, now so near that if she reached out her left arm, she could touch it. . . .

"Isla, for God's sake –" she heard Kyle's voice, and it sounded frightened. Frightened! Now why should a man like Kyle be frightened? He wasn't scared of anything in the world, he'd said that already, he had told her. She felt his hard body as she was lifted and swung against it, and then an awful thing happened, she was being carried *away* from the airstrip jerkily, as though he was running. Then she was flung down so that the breath left her body in a shuddering gasp of pain, and she lay winded, too terrified to scream.

"You were nearly killed. Didn't you hear it?" His voice was ragged with anger, and Isla looked at him.

"Hear what?" It was a croak. She could scarcely speak.

"The plane – about to land – and you – you –" he stopped. His face was white. "You said you'd stay where you were –"

"I thought you were going without me." She struggled to her feet, and he held her. And she saw the small plane, wings shimmering in the sun. Then she knew what Kyle had meant when he said she could have been killed. She had been going straight towards that landing strip. She watched two men getting out, two tiny figures they seemed to her, but the sun on the wings was too dazzling for her to see them clearly.

She heard them shout, but distantly, voices faded and far away. It was all too much. The moment of rescue had come, a wonderful moment, the hope that had been at the back of her mind ever since Kyle's first dreadful words of truth. Her time to escape from him. She had had it all planned in her mind, how she would get away from him once they were off the island, but now it all seemed too much effort. She closed her eyes, the continuing nightmare returning, too weak even to struggle away from his

121

restraining hold.

The men were nearer now, one with a broad grin on his face as he came up, hand outstretched to greet them.

"Kyle!" he said. "I never thought I'd see you here – like this. And how –" but for Isla the moment of reunion was over. Her head went back as she fainted.

She thought she must still be dreaming when she opened her eyes. She was lying in a soft comfortable bed, and there was a sheet over her, a fan moving lazily on the ceiling, so she watched that for a few moments, enjoying the dream, quite different from the nightmares, quite pleasant. . . .

"She is awake." It was a soft voice, a woman's voice, but Isla saw nobody, so she struggled to sit up, because there certainly wasn't another woman on the island. Or was there? It was so confusing, everything was. Because there weren't any beds on the island either, and it was most certainly a comfortable bed, not her imagination.

The girl came forward. Not a woman but a girl of about twelve or thirteen, and she was smiling, her teeth very white in a pretty face. There was something vaguely familiar about her. Isla lay back agin.

"I don't know where I am," she said. "Are we on the island?"

The girl smiled again. "Trintero, yes. My sister has gone to tell Kyle you are awake." Trintero! But that was where they had been before setting out. And then Isla remembered. It all came tumbling back in a jumble of blurred events, all out of sequence, like a giant jig-saw. She looked round at the room – an ordinary bedroom, the furniture plain, white-painted, bright rugs on the tiled red floor.

She spoke to the girl slowly. "Please tell me where I am. Is this somebody's house?"

"You are at my father's hotel. You came with Kyle one day –"

"George's?"

"Yes," the girl nodded. "I am Tina. My sister Lila and I have been watching you." Then came the big shock. Said without a change of tone, the girl was clearly unaware of the effect her words would have on Isla. "You have been here for three days."

"Three days!" Isla clutched at the sheet.

"Why, yes. Is there something wrong? Please –" Tina bit her lip, her pretty face anxious. Clearly she thought she had frightened Isla. She had, but in a way she could not imagine. What if Kyle had contacted her father? What if he were here, or on his way?

"Tina, tell me – what's been the matter with me?" Better to approach it slowly. Isla's wits were working now.

"You have had a bad fever." Tina shrugged prettily. "But you are better now, I can see that."

"I'm sure I am. But I don't remember leaving that island. Do you – do you know anything about where we've been?"

"Oh yes!" Tina's dark brown eyes widened in delight. No wonder her face had seemed so familiar. She was very like her brother, Costas. "You crashed on a deserted island and had to stay there until Kyle managed to get the radio working –"

Now was the time. Now, before anyone returned. "Tina, tell me," Isla reached out an appealing hand and touched the girl's arm, "is anyone here for me – any man?"

"A man?" The girl was clearly puzzled. "There is Kyle –"

"Yes, I know. I mean, anyone else, an older man –?" But before she could finish, she heard a door open, then footsteps, a man's voice, and a woman's. And Kyle Quentin walked into the bedroom, following a taller, slimmer version of Tina.

Isla watched him helplessly. She didn't want to speak to him. She heard the girl say something to Tina, who turned and began to walk away from the bed, and she said: "Wait, Tina –" but Kyle interrupted her.

"I won't be long, girls," he said. His eyes were on Isla. She could read nothing in them. She heard the door close behind them, then he pulled up a chair and sat down.

"And how are you?" he asked.

She turned her head slightly away. "Go away. I don't want to talk to you."

"That attitude won't get you anywhere."

"Won't it?" She turned back to look at him. "Then I'll ask you a question instead. When – when is my father coming?"

His eyes narrowed fractionally. "Why?"

"Why?" Isla clutched the sheet. "You ask me *that*?" Her voice rose slightly. "Do you suppose I've forgotten what you told me on that island? I may have been ill, but I'll never forget *that*. Not as long as I live."

"I'm taking you to him. He's not coming here, Isla."

124

She looked at him, not sure whether to believe him or not. If that were true, there might be a chance. . . .

Nothing must show on her face. He must not be able to guess. "And when are we going?" she asked.

"When you're better."

"Then I'll make sure it's not for a very long time," her voice was dark with bitterness.

"Why fight? To run away like you did, leaving no word – isn't that cruel? Can't you at least go back and talk things over with him and –"

"*Please!*" She turned on him. "Spare me *that*! You don't know anything – you certainly don't know *him* or you wouldn't talk like that. You're just someone he hired to do some dirty work for him – I'm well aware of what kind of man you are," her voice was shaking now, low and intense with the anger welling up inside her, and she saw his face change, saw the harsh deepening lines at the sides of his mouth, and knew she had struck home. Something drove her on. "You acted a part for nearly two weeks to get me liking –" she nearly choked over that word, "liking you. And – you succeeded. Did that m-make you feel good? Tell me, did it?" Unshed tears were bright in her eyes. "I despise you utterly. You're hateful, do you hear me? *Hateful!*" And as he began to stand up, she leaned forward as if fearful that he would move away before she could finish what she had to say. "Can't you listen? Are you running away now?" And then, as he didn't answer: "You expected me to listen, on that island of yours. I had to listen to you telling me those dreadful things. Oh, why did you have to tell me them? Why?"

"I've aready told you. I couldn't go on living the lie. Not there – not when I didn't know how long –" he stopped. He was angry, she knew that, but there was more to it than reaction caused by her words. But she didn't know what it was. Not then.

"Go on. You didn't know how long we'd be there? Is that what you were going to say?"

There was something very disturbing in the air, a throbbing, painful tension, stretched nearly to breaking point. Isla was frightened – of him – as well as of this other indefinable atmosphere. She could scarcely breathe because of it. This man was her enemy, and he could be dangerous, her instinct warned her, and yet she knew she must not give in. She must go on – she *must*. "I'll tell you something now, Kyle Quentin," she said slowly and carefully, because it was important to get this right. "You can't *make* me go with you back to England. Nobody can if I don't want to go. I'm over eighteen, I've not committed any crime, and if you try and get me on to another plane I'll scream blue murder. I shan't – I shan't go anywhere with you, ever again. You are a *brute*."

Without a word, Kyle turned and walked out of the room. Isla lay back, exhausted by her own outburst, frightened at the reaction she had caused in him. He had seemed to be visibly keeping himself in check from answering her. She had seen his hands tighten into fists, almost as if the effort were too great. If she had been a man, he would have struck her, she knew that as surely as if he had told her. "I *hate* him," she whispered, and the fan disturbed the air and took away the sound of the intense words so that they vanished for ever. But even as

126

she said them, Isla knew that they weren't strictly true – but she didn't know why.

It seemed as though Tina had appointed herself as Isla's nurse. She was a pleasant girl, laughter-filled, who clearly worshipped Kyle, for she spoke about him in a certain tone that left Isla in no doubt. She returned a few moments after Kyle had left the room, and there was the slightest of frowns on her forehead. Isla soon found out why.

"Kyle seemed very angry just now. Is everything not all right?" Isla looked at her. How old would she be? Not more than thirteen. Too young to confide in. She shook her head.

"I can't explain, Tina. Yes, he was angry – but it's nothing you need worry about –" she stopped, tears perilously near, and the girl came forward impulsively and flung her arms round Isla in a motherly gesture.

"Oh, please, do not cry. You are not well –"

"I'll be all right in a minute. I'm s-sorry."

"See, maybe you are hungry. I will go and bring some food for you. You would like that?" Isla had to smile, despite the other pain, the pain of bitterness. If only a good meal were the cure for all her troubles!

"Yes, I am hungry. That would be nice. But I don't want to make any work for you –"

"It is my pleasure, truly. Kyle asked if I would help to look after you, and I am happy to do so." The light that shone in her eyes when she said it, told Isla quite plainly of her feelings towards him. Poor girl, she thought. You don't know him.

"Thank you, Tina. You are very kind."

"I shall not be long. And I will fetch back some magazines for you to read. You would like that?"

"Yes, I would like that." She watched the girl leave, and after a moment, curious as to where she might be in the hotel, Isla stepped shakily out of bed. It was a long walk to the window, but she made it and leaned thankfully on the window still to get her breath back. She had a shock. She could see the hotel from where she stood. Not far away, and she could even see Tina speeding along the path like a young gazelle. Then Isla remembered. On her day's visit there with Kyle she had noticed several wooden chalets in the grounds, set among the trees, and he had explained that people often stayed in them when they wanted privacy – they were a particular favourite for honeymooners, he had added, straightfaced. And now she was in one of them herself. She leaned out of the open window and saw another chalet just a few dozen yards away, set at such an angle that privacy was guaranteed. Somehow it made her feel very lonely. How clever of Kyle to make sure she was isolated thus. How very clever of him – and typical. It hardened Isla's resolve to get away from him just as soon as she could. It also gave her an idea. If she could get her strength back without him knowing, so much the better. To do so she might have to take Tina into her confidence. Would it work? That was the big question. She intended to find out very soon. As soon as the girl came back with her meal, in fact. Carefully, still very weak, Isla made her way back to her bed. Already she was feeling a little better. For now, there was hope.

CHAPTER EIGHT

It was quite true. Isla didn't realize just how much better she felt until after she had eaten. She looked at Tina, who waited anxiously, her young face full of concern as she watched the mouthfuls go down. The meal had been very simple, and quite delicious; scallops cooked in cheese sauce, fresh pineapple afterwards.

But it had been sufficient, and Isla smiled at the girl. "I really needed that," she admitted. "I was starving."

"Yes, I know," Tina nodded. "Kyle tried very much to get some milk and brandy down you when you were poorly, and you took very little. He was worried." Yes, he would be, thought Isla wryly. It would have been very inconvenient to his little plans if I'd gone and died on him.

"Worried?" she said. "Well, he won't be now he knows I've had something. I'm so happy that you're here, Tina – yo. 'd make a super nurse, do you know that?"

Tina looked surprised, then laughed, showing her neat white teeth. "Ah! You must tell my father. I wish very much to be a nurse – but *him* –" she shrugged eloquently, "he thinks I am a baby. Me!"

There was no better time to ask. "How old are you?"

"Nearly fifteen – but I look younger, you see, not like Lila. She is very grown up."

"I'm sure he'll let you when you're a bit older, Tina. You are only young, you know. But you can practise on me – in fact you're doing extremely well now. I'm very grateful."

"That is all the thanks I need. See –" she picked up the tray with Isla's plates on. "I will put this outside for one of the boys to collect. There is a bell in the other room, you know."

"I'm in one of the chalets in the gardens, aren't I?"

Tina nodded. "Yes. You would like to see round it? Are you strong enough yet?"

"I'd love to. And yes, I'd like to try anyway."

"Kyle thought it would be quieter for you here. But you have never been alone."

Isla found out a few minutes later just exactly what that sentence meant. She waited until Tina returned, having taken the tray outside, and gingerly climbed out of bed. She was wearing a blue cotton nightdress, cool and pretty, and Tina seeing her glance down at it, explained: "That is Lila's. She has many, and you are both of a similar size – so –"

"You're all so kind. Really, very kind." It was odd how weak she felt now that she was standing up again. Even with the girl's supporting arm around her waist, Isla's legs seemed as wobbly as jelly. Slowly they walked towards the outer room and just inside the door was a chair, to which Tina waved.

"Sit a moment, please." Isla did so well aware of her own limitations. Then she was able to look around her. It was a small living room cheerfully and brightly furnished with a long settee, two dining chairs and a highly polished table, several pictures on the walls, and gay red and white check curtains at the windows.

"Why, it's lovely!" Isla exclaimed. "Really. What a nice place to spend a holiday."

"Yes, it is. And people can eat their meals here, or go up to the house for them. It is just up to them what they do. These chalets are very popular for couples on honeymoon," and Tina blushed slightly as she said it.

Isla smiled. "I'm sure they are. Is there a kitchen as well?"

"Oh yes! You wish me to make you some coffee? That will be fun, hey?"

It seemed as if Tina was determined to look after her – and Isla suspected that she was enjoying her task. She nodded.

"What a lovely idea. May I see the kitchen?" It was as she stood up that she saw the neatly folded blankets and a pillow at the end of the settee. "Tina, are you sleeping here?" she asked, as they walked towards the other room leading off from the one they were in.

Tina looked faintly surprised. "No. My father would not let me."

"Oh. Is Lila?"

Tina laughed. "Ah no, it is Kyle!"

Isla's heart thudded in sudden dismay – and something else she didn't understand. "You mean – *he's* been here every night?"

"Why, yes!" Tina watched her sit in the light cane chair in the kitchen, then crossed to the row of brightly painted cupboards and opened one. She half turned, pausing in her task of searching for coffee. "You could not be alone at night, you see. And then Lila or I would come in the morning, and he would go."

A helpless sensation of rage filled Isla. Was she never to get away from that man? Like some guardian watch-dog, never leaving her alone. Was this all part of his plan? She would soon find out.

"Well, I'm much better now," she said. "He doesn't need to stay here any more, I'm quite sure." And she smiled reassuringly at Tina, who smiled back.

The coffee was made, and it took time, because Tina spun it out, Isla sensed, simply because she enjoyed play-ing at house. She was an attractive girl who would un-doubtedly grow into a beautiful woman. Not vain, that was obvious, even a little shy and unsure of herself, and Isla felt drawn to her. How nice it would be to have a younger sister like that, she thought almost wistfully.

They drank the coffee in the living room, and Tina brought in a tin of tiny sweet biscuits from the kitchen. Isla ate a few, but her mind was too engrossed on the subject of Kyle Quentin for her really to enjoy them. So he thought he would be staying there again tonight, did he? He was in for a shock. A big shock.

She had made a mistake in telling Tina, she discovered later. It wasn't the girl's fault; Isla had made the remark, and presumably Tina had mentioned it to her sister in all innocence when she went up to the house for Isla's even-ing meal.

Whatever the reason, the result was the same. Isla had a sense of foreboding as night fell. For Tina looked at her as they finished their coffee, and said with a smile: "Kyle thinks you must be a lot better to want to be on your own."

"Oh. He knows?" She hid her dismay as well as she could. She should have realized! They were in the bedroom of the chalet. Isla was not in bed; she sat in the one easy chair, a strangely English-looking chintz-covered one, quite out of place on a tropical island, but very comfortable. Tina sat cross-legged on the floor cupping her coffee with both hands, the tin of biscuits by her side. She was always hungry, Isla had discovered, not without amusement.

"Oh yes. He is coming down soon." Isla's lips tightened. Oh, are you? she thought. But the prospect of another argument with him was suddenly distressing. In spite of her determination, she doubted her strength to fight.

The evening was cooler, a welcome breeze teasing the curtains at the windows; in the background soft music from a portable radio filled the room.

It was an old Supremes record, one of Isla's favourites, and the atmosphere was restful and contented. And so soon to be shattered.

There came a knock at the outer door, and they heard Kyle's voice: "All right to come in?"

"No," Isla said quietly, but the word was lost as Tina jumped up, her eagerness only too obvious.

"We are in here, Kyle," she answered, with a quick shy look at Isla. Kyle walked in, and his presence filled the room with sudden vibrant power. I can't fight him, Isla thought – but I'm going to try.

"I'll take you back to the house, Tina," Kyle said, looking at the girl, who shook her head.

"No. The cups – I must wash them."
133

"I'll do it. Come now, your father is waiting. I think visitors have arrived."

"Oh, pooh – them!" the girl shrugged. "I know. My aunt and uncle from the town. Can I stay here?"

Kyle grinned. How different he was when he did that. Isla couldn't help watching him. She was planning what to say, and it was easier when she saw him – sometimes – but not when he had that look about him. . . .

"I don't think he'd appreciate that. He seemed very keen for you to go. That's why I've come early. Come." He reached out and gently took her arm. Then he looked at Isla for the first time since coming in. "I'm watching Tina gets safely in. I'll not be a minute."

They were gone. In the silence that fell, the words of a new tune filled the room, Jim Reeves, a sad song: "Missing You." Isla took a deep breath. She thought suddenly of Maria and Roberto and the boys. They were the only ones she was missing. They must be told that she was all right, for they would be worried. She felt ashamed that she had only just now thought of them; that it had taken a song to remind her. . . .

He came in so quietly that he took her by surprise. She never heard the outer door open at all, just his voice as he came in, and looked at her.

"If you want to get ready for bed, I'll walk round outside for five minutes," he said. Isla pulled the thin cotton kimono a little tighter round her. Now was the moment. Now. If she hesitated. . . .

"Thank you for looking after me at night," she said, trying to speak calmly and slowly, but it was difficult, for the words wanted to tumble out all together – "but I'll be

134

all right tonight. I'm much better now, and I know where the bell is –"

"No," he said.

"What do you mean, no?"

He looked faintly amused, almost smiling. "I should think it's obvious what I mean. I stay here, that's all. Subject closed."

The treacherous, weakening anger started to rise. "But – I don't w-want you to," she began. Oh, how awful to be so helpless! "I don't need you here –"

"You made your feelings quite clear earlier today." His face was a carved mask in the warm light from the only lamp in the corner by the bed. Only his eyes had expression, and it was something she did not understand. "I could hardly have forgotten what you said, but it doesn't make the slightest difference. While you're here you don't sleep alone in this chalet."

"Why? Is it dangerous or something?" she challenged.

"It could be. These grounds are extensive, and George has no patrol of any kind. It's no place for a girl on her own."

"Then why am I here? Why not up at the house?" Her eyes gleamed. She had him there –

"Because it's quieter and pleasanter. You've been ill. That hotel is never quiet. It's virtually open twenty-four hours a day – it's a wonder you don't hear the row from here sometimes –"

"You're lying! You've got another reason –"

Steely cool, his voice cut in, and silenced her effectively. "You must be ill to talk so hysterically. Look at you – cheeks flushed. You're not *fit* to be alone, whatever

135

you may think."

"I *am* – you're doing this simply because y-you're frightened I'll t-try and get away –" it was an effort to talk because of the anger and unhappiness spilling out in a warm flood, and to have to fight back the tears as well was almost too much for Isla. She clutched the arms of the chair and took a deep shuddering breath. Suddenly Kyle came over and she instinctively jerked back in the chair, fearful that he might touch her. "No! Go away. Leave me!"

He stopped abruptly before her. Dark shadows touched his face as he looked down on her, turning it into an inscrutable mask of deep strength and frightening power.

"You're terrified." He said it almost impersonally, as if it did not personally concern either of them. "So how would you fare if a man tried to break in?"

"I'd – I'd scream."

"And who would hear you?"

"The people in the next chalet."

"There is no one." He shook his head gently as if reprimanding a child. "This is the only one occupied. You would be completely alone."

Isla looked up at him. For a moment all personal enmity seemed to fade away. "I'd be quite used to that. I always have been alone." The words were said without bitterness, they were wrung out of her involuntarily; she was hardly aware of having uttered them, and she saw his face change fractionally – and then realized just what she had said. And she wondered why she should tell him.

For a moment, tension filled the air in almost tangible waves; she felt she could reach out and touch them. Then the spell was broken as he moved suddenly away. Isla took a deep breath. What had she seen just then in his face? She put her hand to her throat to feel the pulse that beat rapidly there. She was vibrantly, quiveringly aware, quite suddenly, of the man who was in the room with her. He had moved to the window now, and was looking out, a tall erect giant of a man who was frightened of nothing, and certainly not of burglars. The window was wide open, the air was faintly scented with the memory of flowers, and somewhere far away, an animal cried, as if in pain. So he had passed the previous nights there too, had he? And she had not known. She had not known anything at all, only a jumbled blur of bright frightening dreams that faded too quickly to be remembered afterwards. Perhaps she had called out in her delirium – told him more than he needed to be told. Perhaps – but speculation was useless. He was her enemy. In spite of everything, his apparent concern, it did not alter the facts of what he had done, and was intending to do.

Isla felt suddenly sick. She struggled to stand up. "Will you please go away for a while?" she said. "I'm going to get ready for bed. I might not be able to get rid of you, but at least I don't have to have you here in my bedroom."

She held on to the end of the bed until he had walked out of the room. She waited then until she heard the front door close after him. Then she made her slow way to the bathroom which adjoined her bedroom.

A cool shower refreshed her somewhat, and Isla dressed in the fresh pink nightie which Tina had brought with her meal. A huge moth battered at the closed blinds to be let in, and she turned the bathroom light out quickly on her way back into the bedroom.

Gently, carefully, into bed, the sheets fresh and cool, and the outer door opened, and Kyle came in. Of course! He would have been watching for the bathroom light to go off. I should have left it on, thought Isla, as she lay back. What would he have done then? Waited outside all night? The thought would have been amusing, if only she hadn't felt so wretchedly, terribly lonely and sad. She turned her face into the pillow and closed her eyes. Now, more than ever before, she was determined to get away.

She heard him moving about in the living room and kitchen. Then a tap on the bedroom door, and his voice: "Isla, may I come in for the pots?"

"Yes." She didn't move when he came in, nor when she heard him go out again. She stayed quite still until he shut the door after him and then she sat up and picked a magazine from the bedside table. She knew she would not sleep for a while, and she didn't want to think about what had happened.

For a moment, when she awoke, she wondered if Kyle were playing a trick on her – an unpleasant, shocking trick to make her see that she wasn't capable of looking after herself in the chalet. For she had heard a slight sound, and opened her eyes to see the dark outline of a man standing just outside the window, silhouetted against a black velvet sky. Perhaps it was Kyle himself – but what a horrible thing to do! She hadn't imagined he would *ever* do such a thing. . . . The man slid one silent foot over the windowsill and began to climb in, and Isla sat up in bed.

"Kyle?" she said. Then louder, to let him see she wasn't going to be fooled. "Kyle!" A head turned, a listening head; the curtains moved as he pushed them to one side and came across the room at her in a diving leap that told of something much more than any joke – and Isla screamed. She saw the gleam of his teeth as the man's hand clamped over her mouth, and heard the muffled grunt of anger and pain as she bit on it hard.

The darkness exploded into light as the door burst open and Kyle came in at a rush. The next moment the hand had gone from her mouth as Kyle jerked the man away, and there was the jarring impact of two bodies meeting the floor with force. Isla scrambled out of bed, too frightened to shout, nausea rising in her at the realization that what she had thought of as a joke was very far from one. Blind panic filled her for a few moments, and was washed away by the sight of Kyle's hand holding tightly to the other man's – for that other hand held a knife, a wic! edly silver-bright strip of steel that gleamed in the light – and she remembered the bell in the other room and ran across to reach it, nearly slipping on a rug that had been dislodged by Kyle. There was a crack, a thud; she dared not look round, there wasn't time. But her heart leapt to her mouth with fear. She pressed the bell hard, and jabbed it repeatedly. The awful thing was not knowing whether it worked, for there was no sound here, only at the house – and would someone hear?

"Please – oh, please," she begged. She had to help Kyle. There was a statue on the sideboard, the small figure of a dancer, in wood. She snatched it up and ran back into the bedroom, but already the effort was telling on her; Isla's head swam. She must not faint – and she saw one man leaning over the other one, and raised the statue – and saw that it was Kyle. Kyle! The man on the floor gave a groan and his head went to one side, and she lowered the statue slowly, still unbelieving, still not sure – until Kyle spoke:

"Have you rung the bell?" he said. There was blood on his face, the shirt he wore was torn, ripped right down the front – or was it a pyjama top?

Isla took a deep breath, leaning against a chair as her legs threatened to give way beneath her.

"I – I – thought it was you playing a trick," she said, not knowing why she should tell him such a thing, unless perhaps the first memory was still so strong and vivid that it refused to go away. Kyle straightened up, brushed a hand across his cheek, looked at the blood as if mildly surprised, and then at Isla.

"Did you? You would, though, wouldn't you?" He wasn't angry, it was said quite calmly. Isla sat on the bed.

"I'm sorry," she answered. "Yes, I've rung the bell." She put the statue beside her before she dropped it. The room shifted and swayed gently, but she wasn't going to faint – she must not. Not now.

Running footsteps, coming nearer, the outer door crashing open, then George and Costas were in the bedroom, crossing it, looking down at the man on the floor, and George clapped Kyle's shoulder.

"My God! You've done it, my friend," he announced. "It *is* – isn't it?" he turned to Costas, who tore his eyes away from Isla to look at the inert man.

"I am sure – yes." Costas nodded and looked at Kyle,

140

eyes widening in what looked like respect. "What happened?"

"Isla shouted – I came in to see him attacking her." He bent and picked up the knife which had skidded several feet away. He held it up. "Look at that. I bet the poor devil was only after food."

Poor devil! – Isla looked at him. She didn't understand what was happening, only that it wasn't a bad dream, it was real. Costs's hand on her shoulder was solid enough too as he said: "Isla – you wish for a drink of something?"

"Please. What – what is it? Who is he?"

George answered. He and Kyle were busy lifting the man up. Still semi-conscious, he didn't struggle. His body was limp and obviously heavy. "Four days ago he escaped from the prison at the other end of the island. It was better not to tell you – but these things are very worrying." They were going towards the door. The man's feet dragged on the floor and caught in the rug, and Kyle muttered something, then leaned down and hoisted the man in a fireman's lift over his shoulder.

"We'll get him up to the house, George."

She watched them go out, George moving ahead to open doors, to clear the way. Isla sat very still, her hands clammy and cold. She heard someone moving in the other room, but they'd gone. Her heart leapt in sudden renewed fear – and Costas walked in.

"Costas!" The word was a croak of relief.

He came over to her and sat beside her on the bed. "Here, drink this. It is orange juice. I will bring you something stronger if you wish –"

"No!" Alarmed, she clutched his arm. "Don't leave me –"

"Ah no, I would not." His eyes were warm upon her, filled with that look she had seen before, when they had been dancing. As if it was the most natural thing in the world, he put his arm round her shoulder in a protective gesture. "See, I will stay with you, do not worry, Isla."

The orange juice was cold and refreshing, his arm was very comforting, and she let her tensed-up muscles relax. He took the half empty glass from her and put it down on the bedside table. "You are shaking," he said after a moment.

"I'm only just recovering from the shock," she admitted. "If Kyle hadn't been there –" she stopped as she remembered the way she had argued, had told him she didn't need *him*. He hadn't argued back, merely told her he was staying – he could have told her why, but he hadn't.

"Yes – but better not to think about it. It is all over now. All over." His voice was as soothing as the arm which held her and seemed to be imperceptibly tightening around her. And Isla looked up at him, and his face was very near. Very near. Coming nearer, in fact. Then his lips were brushing her cheek, and his voice was husky as he murmured: "You are very lovely, Isla."

She stirred, slightly uneasy, not knowing why. "No –" she began, but the rest of what she was going to say was lost as his lips found hers in a long gentle kiss. He drew away, and what she saw in his eyes made her catch her breath quickly. "Costas – I don't think –"

"I would have liked to have looked after you," he said

very softly. "But Kyle – ah!" an expressive shrug. "That is the problem, no?"

Problem! What a word to use to describe Kyle. How accurate – but not quite in the way that Costas intended, she knew that. And she wondered suddenly just how much Costas did know. There wasn't much time to find out. Kyle could return at any minute.

"Costas," she said quietly, "what has Kyle told you about me?"

He seemed puzzled for a moment, and she added quickly: "I mean, has he said why I'm here – why we got stuck on the island in the first place?"

A slight frown. "You – you were on holiday, yes? And going to visit some other island on business?" He was hesitant. Clearly he knew nothing, for Isla didn't doubt that something would have shown in his tone if he had the slightest inkling of Kyle's true motives. In a way, it made what she had to tell all the more difficult. Who would believe such an incredible tale?

"Costas," she began, "I need help – I have a lot to tell you – but I'm afraid Kyle will be back in a minute. I must get away from him." In her agitation she turned and put her hand on his shoulder. "Please believe me. He's trying to take me back to –" She drew in breath sharply as footsteps crunched on the path outside. "Please – come down during the day. I must talk to you."

She stood up as Kyle entered the living room. Costas stood more slowly. Had he understood? Then he gave her a quick secret nod.

"Yes." It was a mere whisper, but enough. Her heart lifted.

Kyle looked at them as if he guessed what had passed – but he couldn't have, of course, she thought. It was just her over-active imagination.

"Your father has sent for the police," he said, speaking to Costas. "They'll be here soon. We've got our friend tied up." Then he looked at Isla. "I've brought some brandy back. A drop will do you good."

"I will go back." Costas turned and looked at Isla, his back to Kyle for a moment. There was no doubt about the expression on his face now. "Good night, Isla – Kyle," he said. "I am sure there will be no more trouble now." And he went out, moving quickly and quietly. Not as tall as Kyle, yet there was a quiet strength about him, and a kind of confidence. And what was it he had said? "I would lie to look after you." Perhaps he would. She looked at Kyle, about to return to the living room, and after a moment's hesitation, followed him. It would be better if she didn't appear too antagonistic towards him – Not now. And yet she mustn't lean too far the other way, for Kyle was far shrewder than she had imagined, and would suspect it if she became pleasant.

She watched him pour brandy into two glasses. He handed her one.

"Cheers."

"Cheers. And – thank you."

He lifted one cynical eyebrow. "Don't feel obliged to thank me. It was, as they say, nothing." He had a plaster on his cheek. He might not have been in a fight at all, except for that one small evidence of a cut.

"Why didn't you tell me about the man escaping from prison?"

"Why? I saw no point in alarming you unnecessarily. It was only a remote chance that he'd be anywhere near here, but I don't court danger. You needed protection, it's as simple as that."

There was no getting the better of a man like that. He had answers for everything. And yet there was one thing. He couldn't know that Isla had an ally. For of that fact she was quite certain – Costas would not refuse to help her. She knew that as surely as she knew her own name. She had the feeling that she would sleep soundly in her bed for the rest of the night. In spite of all that had happened, there was now a small quiet certainty of escape from Kyle. And very soon.

CHAPTER NINE

THE morning came, bright sunlight bursting through the windows as if to clear away the last vestiges of night, and the terror that had so nearly been. Isla woke from a deep sound sleep to hear voices in the other room. She lay for a moment listening to them. Was it Costas? Surely he wouldn't come while Kyle was still there? But one of the voices was a girl's. She heard the light laugh, and relaxed slightly. It was Tina.

Then came Kyle's deeper, answering response. She wondered what they were talking about. Her bedroom door had been left ajar, and there came a light tap, and Tina's head popped round. Her eyes were alight with mischief.

"Isla? May I come in?"

"Yes, of course." Isla sat up.

"What a terrible thing to happen!" Tina's face belied her words. Clearly this was drama, and as such, to be enjoyed. Tina sat on the end of the bed and looked at Isla, as if there might be some change in her, some evidence of the things that had happened. "You must have been very frightened."

"I was. But Kyle was there. He heard me shout."

"I know – Costas has told me. The man has gone – the police came and took him away in a van." She sighed. "I was asleep – it was during the night."

Isla had to smile. "Oh, Tina, did you expect them to

146

wake you up?"

The girl shook her head. "Oh dear! Of course not. But - well, I miss everything." Her brown eyes widened. "Did you know what he was in prison for? He had stolen a lot of money, *and* –"

"No! I think that's enough." Kyle's voice came from the doorway. He sounded stern, but was smiling at Tina, as if to take any reprimand from the words.

Tina pulled a face at him. "Oh! You are cross?"

"No. But Isla isn't well enough yet, I don't think." Isla was immediately intrigued. What could it be that she wasn't supposed to know? Later there would be an opportunity – when he had gone. She could wait.

Kyle was carrying a glass, the outside frosted as if the contents were cold. He handed it to Isla. "Fresh grapefruit juice. Someone is bringing you breakfast down in a few minutes."

"Thank you." He looked as if he wasn't long out of bed. Although dressed, he obviously had to wait for a wash and shave until he went to the house, for the only bathroom in the chalet led off from Isla's bedroom. He still wore the plaster, and his hair was spiky and untidy. He looked formidable and tough, and her heart skipped a beat. *Could* she get away from him? Then she remembered something important.

"Maria!" she exclaimed, and Tina looked puzzled. "I must let Maria know –"

"Yes. I have already done so. She was naturally worried. Now she knows you're safe." But does she know about *you*? Isla thought, as she watched him standing there in the room. How did you manage that, I wonder?

147

She would have to tread carefully now.

"I'd like to phone her myself," she said, in a very casual voice, fearful of giving anything away.

"The lines are very bad from here. I had an awful lot of trouble getting through," he answered, smoothly, quickly – too quickly. Was he lying?

Their eyes met. Tina was excluded from this exchange that only they knew about. Perhaps she sensed the atmosphere, though, for a slight frown touched her forehead as she glanced quickly, first at Isla, then at Kyle. His face gave nothing away to the casual observer. Only Isla saw the hard bleak look about his eyes – the look she knew so well. She would not get past that defence. Better not to try now – not with Tina there.

Kyle, as if knowing, turned to Tina. "Will you go and see if they are coming down with the food yet?" he asked her. "I want to talk to Isla a minute."

"Yes," she nodded, then ran out. They waited until the outer door slammed, and then Isla spoke. And she knew he was waiting for it. "Why don't you want me to talk to Maria?" she demanded.

"Did I give you that impression?"

"Yes, you damn well did. And can't you give a straightforward answer to any questions I ask?"

"I told you – the lines are bad from here. George will tell you that as well."

"Oh, I dare say he would. You men stick together, don't you?" she asked bitterly.

"You're still overwrought. How do you think Maria would feel if you poured all your troubles out to her –"

"So at least you admit I've *got* troubles," she flashed.

"Haven't we all?" It was said lightly, but there was an underlying thread running through his voice. It triggered off Isla's temper.

Heedless of what he might say or do, she got out of bed and pulled on the cotton housecoat that Lila had lent to her. There was always the sense of being at a disadvantage when she was in bed. And she had something to say.

"Listen," she breathed. "Who the hell do you think you are? You're keeping me a p-prisoner here – like that man – only he escaped, didn't he?" She stood in front of him, her bosom heaving with the temper that filled her. "I know why you brought me here to George's, and not to the town. It's to keep me out of the way. *And* I know why you wanted me to stay in this chalet – and have Tina looking after me – you don't care who you use, do you?" Her cheeks were flushed, her eyes sparked fire and she no longer cared – she wasn't frightened of him – at that moment. "She's just a girl – and she likes you, she actually likes you! My God, she doesn't know you, does she? And now – now you won't let me phone my friend Maria –" she faltered, the impetus that carried her so far weakening as her own lack of strength, and the force of her words, took its toll.

"Take it easy –" he began, and reached out his arm as if to try and soothe her.

"Don't *touch* me." She lashed out and knocked his arm away. He was hateful! He stood there, exuding an air of complete calm, as if they were discussing the weather, when Isla felt as if her own future life was at stake, as if everything depended on this man, this awful man. Her fists clenched as a surge of helpless anger swept through

149

her. And then he laughed. He actually *laughed*.

That did it. Isla's control finally snapped. She swung one upraised fist at his face and followed it with the other, to pummel him with all her strength. He turned slightly sideways to dodge the full force of the blows, moving so swiftly and easily that it caught her off balance. Just for the split second – but it was enough. The next moment she was caught and held – and he looked down at her, and he wasn't laughing any more. One hand clamped on each of her wrists, not tight enough to hurt, but firmly enough to make her feel utterly helpless, and he wasn't calm any more either, she could see that.

"Listen, you little wildcat," he said. "If you go around swinging punches like that you could land in trouble. They're not all like me, you know."

"No, thank God!" she gasped. "There can't be many men who'd do your job – no matter what the money. Who would do what you did – sweet-talked me into trusting you – liking you. I did, you know – I thought you were – were –" she faltered, but she had to go on now. "I thought you were s-super –" she tried to pull her hands free of his grasp, but the grip tightened imperceptibly, just enough to let her know that he wasn't prepared to let her go.

"You're hurting me!" she gasped.

"No, I'm not. You're hurting yourself – by fighting me. It won't do you any good –"

"I hate you!"

"Perhaps you do. Do you think I care?" Hard, cynical – yet the words were harsh, almost angry. They made her look sharply up at him, jolted her out of her own anger.

What she saw in his face made her gasp. There was something in his eyes – something – but what it was she didn't know. The anger that had overcome her fear was receding, leaving in its place a quieter despair. He was a man without mercy. Had she actually hoped that he would change his mind – ever? The hope was gone now. There was only Costas. He must help her, he *must*.

She closed her eyes, and waited for him to release her. Which he did – because the outer door opened, very noisily. But Isla was left with the strange impression that he had been about to say something. She would never know what it was, if in fact he had been going to at all, but the sensation persisted for quite a while after, until it was forgotten.

Later that day Isla and Tina went for a short walk outside the chalet. Kyle had gone before Isla even started her breakfast, leaving abruptly, without another word.

Tina's eyes had widened on seeing him go, and she had carried the tray into the bedroom and looked at Isla.

"Kyle – he is angry?" she ventured.

"Yes." Isla badly needed someone to confide in, to share the overwhelming depression that now filled her. "Oh yes, but I don't suppose you know why, do you?"

"He loves you – and you do not love him?"

The idea was so preposterous that Isla could do nothing except stare in wonderment at Tina. Was that what she thought? She couldn't even bring herself to tell the girl, she was too full for words. Then – but not later. She had made some reply, she forgot after what it was, but when they were walking, in the sunny gardens near that

151

quiet chalet, Isla knew she must tell Tina. Not all the story, but enough to make her understand some of the misery that now overwhelmed her.

There was a long wooden seat in the shade of some very tall elegant palms. "Can we sit here for a minute, Tina?" Isla asked. It was odd how tired you could be after a few days in bed, and even a short walk had taxed her strength.

"Of course. You wish to go back?"

"Not yet. It's lovely here – it's very kind of you to spend all this time with me," Isla said, smiling as Tina sat beside her.

"No, I enjoy it. Since I am on holidays there is not much for me to do – and my father finds jobs for me in the hotel where I am bored." She pulled a little face. "This is much better, I think."

Isla laughed. "Yes, I see what you mean." Then she sighed. What a mess it all was!

"Oh, Tina," she said, "I wish I could tell you –" she stopped. How could she begin?

"Yes?" The girl's eyes widened. "You can tell me what you like. You think I am maybe too young to understand? I know there is trouble between you and Kyle – I can see that much. But I don't know what it is."

"It's a long story. You're right about there being trouble with Kyle and me – but I know that you like him –" she paused. This was difficult.

"Yes, I like him." Tina's face was very expressive. "He is always kind to me – and always has been, ever since I was small. He is a nice man."

"To you, maybe." Isla could believe it. He had always

152

been good with Maria's three boys, in the brief acquaintance in Rio. Perhaps that hadn't been an act; some men genuinely did like children; even ones as unlikely as Kyle.

"But I can see – I can tell that things are not right." Tina put her hand on Isla's arm as if to reassure her. "Please don't think I am being nosey. But if it will help you to tell me, please do so. I am very grown up," she added, tilting her head proudly.

Isla gave her a gentle smile. "I think you are – truly, you will make a very good nurse, Tina – you have that understanding that is needed. I'll tell you – but I warn you, you may find it hard to believe."

"Then try me."

"It's simply this. I was working in Rio when I met Kyle –" and so Isla began the story of the events that had begun one happy carefree day on Copacabana beach, and culminated in her second arrival on Trintero Island, as a guest in Tina's father's hotel.

Tina listened in silence, and when Isla had finished, she didn't speak for a few moments. Then, slowly, hesitantly, she said: "Oh, Isla – I am so sorry, so very sorry. I could not imagine –" She stopped.

"It's true, every word. Now you see why I must get away from here. I too am sorry to have to tell you these things about a man you like so much – but I feel so helpless. I feel so – alone." Isla looked down at her hands, fighting back the tears of weakness.

"And you want Costas to help you," Tina said thoughtfully. "I can tell you now – he likes you very much, Isla – *very* much. But he thought that Kyle was – was –" she stopped, biting her lip.

153

"Was in love with me?" Isla softly finished it for her. "And nothing could be further from the truth, I'm afraid. I'm just a – a parcel to be delivered safely somewhere to *him*." The bitterness was in that word.

"You are too weak to go just yet." Tina was fast recovering from any shock at Isla's story, that was clear. "It would not be wise. But both Costas and I will help you – don't worry about that." She spoke decisively, and Isla looked at her, marvelling at the maturity she had sensed in that young face.

"I feel so much better now," she admitted. "Telling you has done me good, really. It just seemed as if I was completely alone before, without anyone to tell. And now I have two friends." She smiled, shaking her head at the thought.

"I will tell Costas what you have told me. We will work out something, don't worry." And then Tina looked full into Isla's eyes. "It is difficult to believe such bad things of Kyle – but I know that what you say is true. And you can trust me. *I* will not let him take you away." Her mouth compressed into a tight line, a determined line, and she nodded as well, as if to confirm the decision.

"I thought that if I could get my strength back – without letting him know –" Isla began.

"Yes! That is good. Don't worry. I will make it seem that you are very weak. He will not guess – and all the time you will be getting stronger. Yes! I like that." Tina's eyes shone. "We can pretend you are not eating – but I will bring you extra food, things to help you grow strong – and we won't tell him. So he will not even imagine you are getting better. And we will go little walks every day when Kyle will not be here. I can spy on him too – he will not know I am watching him at all. Then, when you are properly better, we will take you to Trintero airport and you can fly to Rio."

It was incredible, the way her mind had adjusted to the new situation, thought Isla. She had felt the need for a confidante – she had not imagined such a response as this. But she still felt guilty at having shattered the girl's illusions about the man she had so clearly thought wonderful. "Tina," she said, "perhaps Kyle had a very *good* reason for doing what he did," she didn't believe it herself, even as she said the words, but she had to try to soften the blow somewhat.

"Perhaps he did," the girl shrugged. "But I can't imagine what it could be – can you?"

"No," Isla had to admit. "But –"

"No, please. I know what you are trying to say. It is all right, Isla, truly. These things happen. People are not always what they seem." Which was, Isla thought, a remarkably profound statement from such a young girl. And one she was to recall – but only much later.

So the little plan went into action, and Isla felt better than she had done for a while. Later that day, Costas came down to the chalet. Isla and Tina were playing chess – or rather Tina was trying to teach Isla. It was one game she had never been remotely interested in, because it had always seemed too complicated to bother about. Now, with the two of them giggling like a pair of schoolgirls as Tina tried to explain the various rules and moves, it began to seem almost fun.

Costas came quietly in and stood watching them by the door before Isla looked up and saw him. Immediately she felt confused, wondering what he would be thinking. Tina had explained very briefly at lunch that she had told Costas the situation, and that he was very concerned, and would be down as soon as he could get away. And now here he was. One look into his eyes told Isla what she needed to know. Relief flooded her.

"Hello," he said quietly. "Kyle has just gone into the town, so we can talk. I do not think he will be back for some time." He sat on the arm of the settee. "Don't let me interrupt your game."

"You're not. Tina's trying to teach me. We can come back to it later." She turned sideways to look more clearly at him. "Do you know everything?"

"Yes." He nodded. "There is no problem. We will help you as much as we can." He paused. "Kyle was worried that you left so much lunch." A faint smile. "So the little plan seems to be working."

Isla and Tina looked at each other. It had seemed a waste to leave a tray of delicious food virtually untouched, and Isla had felt guilty about it, but if it was having an effect like that . . .

"But how did you smuggle the other food out to me without any questions?" Isla wanted to know.

"Pooh!" Tina laughed and shrugged. "That is no problem. Paul, the youngest chef, will do *anything* for me. I told him I was *starving*, and he gave me that most delicious fish."

It had been delicious too, thought Isla, cooked in a light fluffy sauce, and she had eaten every scrap. Young

Paul sounded an interesting person to know.

"So we are all right for the meals. Of course, you must eat something off your tray — or you would die if you were getting nothing. But I will make sure that Kyle sees what you leave," Tina finished.

Costas nodded. "Yes. And I am checking on flights to Kingston, and what connection you need for Rio."

"Money!" Isla exclaimed. "I didn't bring much with me. Not enough for plane fares, anyway." She put her hand to her face in dismay. If all the plans should come to nothing because of that!

Costas looked at Tina, then said hesitantly: "I have enough — I will have to go to the bank in town —"

"No! I can't let you do that." Then Isla remembered. "My watch! Are there such things as pawnshops — you know, where they will give you money on a valuable item — or even if they would buy them?"

Costas looked doubtful, then nodded. "Yes, I think so. I will try for you —"

"It's in my case. I'll get it." Isla went into the bedroom and took her wristwatch from its box. She had not bothered to wear it since staying on the island. She carried it back and handed it to Costas. "It's an Omega I had for my eighteenth birthday. It's worth at least five hundred pounds."

He handled it with care, and Tina looked at the delicate watch, the face surrounded by diamonds, the strap solid white gold in a simple yet beautiful design.

"Oh, Isla, it's lovely! May I try it on?" she breathed.

"Of course," Isla smiled. On an impulse she said: "Just a moment," and returned to the bedroom. On her dressing table was a bracelet, also a present from her father. She took it back to the girl. "Try that on your other wrist."

She helped Tina to fasten the delicate platinum bracelet with its amethysts gleaming softly in the light. "Do you like it?"

Tina sighed. "Ah yes! You are lucky, Isla."

Lucky? Isla thought. If possessions make you lucky, then maybe I am – but what empty things when they are given without love. To her father they had been merely visible evidence of wealth. She did not treasure them. They meant nothing to her.

"The bracelet is yours –" then as Tina would have protested, she added: "I want you to have it for all your help. Please, Tina, it would give me great pleasure if you accepted."

"Then I will. Thank you, Isla." The girl flung her arms impulsively round Isla and hugged her. Costas watched them and smiled slightly, but said nothing. It seemed to Isla, all of a sudden, as if events were moving to a conclusion. A pattern was beginning to emerge from all that was happening, everything fitting into place, and moving forward gently and inexorably. She wondered how soon it would be before she was able to leave Trintero, and asked Costas, who answered, after a few moments' thought: "I think in about a week, if things go as they are now."

A week! One more week of Kyle, and then to be rid of him for ever. Her heart lifted. Seven days more of deception, and then goodbye. Isla sighed, for a sudden chill touched her, and she didn't understand it and looked around to see if there was a breeze, but there was none.

"That will be wonderful," she said, then added hastily: "Even though I don't want to leave you both. But I promise I will come back one day soon." Tina nodded, smiling. "Yes. And we will write – please, Isla?"

"Of course." There was a lump in Isla's throat and it refused to go away. How nice to find real friends – and how sad to have to leave them so soon. She turned away lest they should see. "Let me make coffee," she said, with an effort at brightness. And she went into the kitchen, and didn't see the look exchanged by brother and sister – a look that was almost one of pity.

The next few days passed quietly, and almost exactly as planned. Isla was eating well – and yet it seemed that her appetite was poor, for the trays of food were sent back to the hotel with almost as much on them as when they came. Isla and Tina took longer walks each day, and Isla knew that she was nearly well again, for she was no longer tired, even on the furthest stretches of their walks.

The two girls got on well, and now that Isla had told Tina the truth, she was able to speak more fully about her life in London, and latterly in Rio. She had written a letter to Maria, telling her the full story of Kyle, his deception, and her adventures, and she had finished by telling Maria that she was planning to return as soon as she was strong enough to travel. On the rare occasions that she saw Kyle, Isla was cool yet polite. The knowledge that she was so soon going should have been a joy in her heart. Most strangely, it was not. She didn't understand it. She only knew that his presence disturbed and distressed her, and it was always a relief to have Tina there with her whenever he was about.

On Wednesday evening he came into the chalet as she and Tina sat listening to the radio, sipping long sharp drinks of fresh lime and ice. It was dark, and he had taken to coming for the night fairly late, usually when Isla was in the bedroom. She and Tina were still in the living room when his knock came at the door. They looked at one another, then Isla spoke.

"Come in."

It was quite a shock to see him. He looked either as if he had been drinking, or was tired. Faint shadows were under his eyes, his mouth unsmiling, even when he looked at Tina.

"You're early," Isla said. "We're listening to the radio."

"I know. But I haven't managed to speak to you for a few days. You're not eating your food. Are you not well?"

She dared not look at Tina, lest they gave the whole thing away. She shrugged. "I'm all right. Just not hungry." She looked coolly at him. "Why?"

"You need to eat properly."

"Thank you for your concern, which I find very touching." She didn't trouble to hide the sarcasm. There was within her the terrible urge to hurt him, as he had hurt her. She wasn't prepared for what he would say next.

"I'm going to call in a doctor to see you," he said.

She absorbed the shock quickly. "I won't see him if you do – is this what's known as protecting your investment?" She saw the flash of something in his eyes – yet it wasn't anger, it was far more disturbing, and she took a quick breath.

Tina stood up. "I shall go back to the hotel, I think." She looked at Isla. "Or do you wish me to stay?"

"No, thanks, Tina. I've enjoyed your company today. Thank you for coming down again." Tina smiled. "I'll be here in the morning. Perhaps we might try a little walk around the chalets?" Her back was to Kyle, and she gave Isla a mischievous wink as she said it.

"That would be nice – I think I might manage it." They had made sure that Kyle was well out of the way before they set off on their long walks. And if he believed about the food. . . .

"I'll watch you back."

Tina turned to him. "Thank you, Kyle. You *are* kind." She had changed towards him since Isla's revelations. It was inevitable, Isla supposed, but she didn't feel happy about it, and she knew Kyle was well aware of the difference in the girl. It was as if she had suddenly grown up. She was subtly cooler, the air of puppyish friendliness all gone, vanished for ever. She watched them go out of the door. Costas had taken the watch into the town and returned with a receipt and three hundred pounds. He had also brought back timetables from the airport on Trintero. There was a flight on Friday to Kingston, Jamaica. An overnight stop there, and a journey the following day which would take her to Rio de Janeiro.

It was settled. Her ticket was in her bag, plus the change from the pawning of her watch. All she had to do now was wait. Wait.

And Kyle came back at that moment, even as she said

161

the word to herself. For a moment it seemed as if she might have said the word aloud, for Kyle's glance was sharp on her. He shut the door behind him.

"All right," he said. "Get it off your chest."

Isla lifted her eyebrows. "What a crude expression! What exactly do you mean?"

"You know damn well. Why the hell aren't you eating? Dieting, or hunger strike?"

"Neither," Isla retorted crisply. "I can't help it if I can't eat, can I?"

"You'll never get your strength back."

"And I bet that worries you, doesn't it? Oh, how touched I am! You'll excuse me now, I want to go to bed. You will agree that sleep is equally important in restoring one's strength. Good night." She turned and walked out of the living room into the bedroom, careful not to take the short journey at too brisk a pace. At the door, just before she closed it behind her, she turned round to look at Kyle. What she saw caused her to catch her breath sharply. For a moment she thought he must be in terrible pain. There was a look of agony on that usually inscrutable face. I don't care, she thought – and went in and slammed the door. But the image of his face lingered for quite a few seconds, and it wasn't until she heard him moving about, heard the radio switched on again, that she moved away from the door. She went into the bathroom and closed the door. In two days I'll be free, she thought. Free – away from here, and him. Her hand faltered and stopped as she was about to reach out and switch on the shower. She watched it. Her hand was trembling and she wanted to cry. But she did not know why.

CHAPTER TEN

THE next day there was a bad storm. It started early, just before dawn when everything is still black and silent and lonely. Isla had been woken by some other noise – a sound from the living room, and had lain awake for several seconds, heart fast beating at the remembrance of those other sounds not so long ago when an escaped prisoner had tried to attack her. The noises were faint, but not frightening. After a few minutes she crept to the door and put her ear to it. The sounds were instantly magnified – faint footsteps, the even more distant strains of the radio, the chink of glass meeting table. Then a soft scrape – a match being lit, surely. So Kyle was awake, having a drink and a smoke and listening to music. Isla crept to her bedside clock, which showed a quarter to four. The air was very heavy, almost sultry, and she knew she would have difficulty getting to sleep again. Perhaps that was why he had woken. She went and lay on top of the bed, just lay quietly thinking about a lot of things.

It was almost a relief to hear the thunder following the brilliant blue flash of sheet lightning from outside. Isla flinched, her memories of storms particularly vivid and painful. She had been in two storms already with Kyle. This was the third – and undoubtedly the last.

She sat up as the blue flame rippled round the chalet, seeming to touch its wall with electric fire. She was only slightly frightened, but there were a lot of tall trees nearby. She clasped her hands tightly together, waiting for the next, inevitable flash.

"Isla?" A rapping at her door. She didn't answer, then when it came again she got out of bed, went to the door and opened it.

"Yes?"

"I thought you might be nervous."

"I'm all right," but the next rippling flash, seeming to surround them, belied her words and she flinched, the expression showing only too clearly on her face.

"Come out here and have a drink." The thunder almost drowned his words, and she turned and ran back to the bed for her cotton wrap. When she went back into the living room, he had vanished. Sounds came from the kitchen, then he reappeared carrying a filled glass which he handed to her. He was fully dressed, in jeans and blue shirt and flat rope sandals. And there was something about him. . . . Isla caught her breath. What was it? There was an atmosphere, not caused by the storm she knew, a tension that vibrated around them. Kyle was watching her now.

"Cigarette?"

She shook her head. "No, thanks." She looked down at her glass, at the clear greeny liquid, the ice floating on the top. Cool lime. And thunder rumbled round outside, leaving them in this oasis of comparative quiet – yet with its tense atmosphere which was making her more uneasy by the minute.

"The trees –" she began. Anything to dispel the awful pressure building up inside her.

"Yes. I've been outside and looked. These chalets have

164

been carefully placed – the trees might look very near, but even if one was struck, it wouldn't fall on us."

"How can you be sure?" She looked at him then, slightly scornful.

"I can. And I am. Want to go out and see for yourself?"

"No." Nothing would induce her to go outside in *this*.

"Well, you'll just have to take my word for it, won't you?" There was an edge to his voice, one she hadn't heard before. It was as if he were under a strain. She didn't imagine it was the storm. He had shown no fear before – not even during their disastrous plane trip. So it wasn't that. But what was it? More and more she was coming to realize what a deeply complex character he was.

"Is that supposed to reassure me?" She gave a bitter laugh. She had to stop speaking as a clap of thunder came almost on the heels of another flash. It was now right overhead, the ground beneath them shaking with the force of the storm. Then the rain started suddenly, abruptly, drumming on the roof and walls, lashing down the windows in a mounting crescendo of sound that was suddenly frightening.

Isla stood up nervously, unable to sit there any longer, too restless to be still – yet with nowhere to escape. There was a sense of imprisonment in that room, and she wanted to burst out: "I'm going – I'm *escaping* from you – and I'm glad! Do you hear me? Glad!" But the words stayed in her head, not to be spoken. Ever. She felt almost ill. She put her hand to her forehead. She mustn't become ill again now. Not now – not when escape was so near, so soon.

"You'd better go back to bed." His voice cut in. He spoke like a stranger. "You'll only upset yourself staying here with me."

"Will I?" She turned on him. "And whose fault will that be?" The ragged edge of her temper flared. Her eyes were large and lustrous, her hair tousled still from sleep; and she looked beautiful. But she didn't know that, she wasn't concerned with herself, only with the man standing there with her in the room.

He didn't answer, and she went over and stood before him. "Answer me," she cried. "Are you a coward? Can't you say anything?"

"I could say a lot – but you wouldn't want to hear." His voice held a tinge of bitterness.

"Try me."

He turned abruptly away and stuck his hands in his pockets. "Get back to your bedroom," he said harshly.

"I'm damned if I will. You asked me out. You can't give me orders any more. Do you hear me? I don't have to do what you tell me – you have no –"

She gasped as he turned back again, whirling swiftly, lightly round and taking hold of her arms. "Ow! Let me –"

He took her completely by surprise. Whatever she had expected it had not been this. His mouth came down on hers in a savagely brutal kiss, a hungry searching of lips that startled and frightened – and finally stirred her, with a deep responsive excitement, a pulsating torment because she hated him, but she had never been kissed like that before. Never.. . .

166

She struggled – briefly. As well to struggle against a force much stronger than anything she had ever encountered. His arms crushed her now; she could not move, or fight, but worse, she didn't even *want* to, that was the awful thing.

The kiss changed; it was no longer brutal, it was deep and full of passion, and Isla knew this difference, but she didn't know why it was so. Then sanity returned – she struggled again, and this time he released her. With a faint cry of horror she flung away from him and ran into her bedroom. Horror – at herself. She slammed and bolted the door and leant against it, trembling as though in a fever, shaking at the reaction that Kyle had aroused so suddenly and helplessly within her. She put the back of her hand to her mouth, pressing hard as if to erase the memory of something terrible. But it hadn't been terrible – and that realization was strangely shocking to her. Her body was still weak and limp from his embrace. How – why – had he dared so?

That question could never be asked. Yet how could she ignore it; pretend that it hadn't happened? And still the storm thundered and growled outside. And she knew something else now. Never again, as long as she lived, would she live through a storm without remembering Kyle.

The storm – but not the memories of it – had gone before breakfast. When Tina called out: "Isla? Are you there?" and came in with the tray, there was no sign of Kyle at all. He might never have been there. The living room was tidy, all evidence of his occupation gone.

Tina looked at Isla as she came out of the bedroom. "Were you frightened in that awful storm?" she asked, concern all over her face.

"A little," Isla admitted. She could never tell anybody what had happened. She still had not recovered from the events.

"We must pack some time today," Tina went on, busily setting the food out on the kitchen table. "I – we – will miss you when you are gone."

Isla gave a faint smile. "I'll miss you. But we'll write. Will your father let you visit me in Rio?"

Tina's eyes shone. "I hope so. Perhaps. I will talk to him."

Isla didn't have to pretend about the food. She really had no appetite at all. Tina made coffee and sat opposite her at the kitchen table.

"You are *sure* you are all right?" she asked.

"I didn't sleep very well," Isla answered. That was true anyway. There had been no sleep for her after the scene with Kyle, merely a lying wait on top of the bed, listening to the thunder dying away, and thinking, forever thinking, until she feared she would go mad with her own thoughts.

"We will go for a long walk today, then you must rest this afternoon. Then we will pack."

"What time must we leave tomorrow?" Isla asked.

"Costas thinks early is best. But not too early. Better to wait until Kyle is safely away at the house. He will have a car ready – hidden – near the gate. He will come for your case and put it in the car. Then, when all is clear, we will walk to the car, and he will drive you to the airport. Once you are there it will be easy to wait in the restaurant or lounge."

"You are both so good. But won't Costas be missed? I don't want to get either of you into trouble –" Isla faltered.

Tina put her hand over Isla's. "Don't worry. Please don't worry. Costas has already fixed some time off to take you – my father thinks he is buying food and drink – he will do that when your plane leaves. I wish I could come too – but I must stay here, out of the way, as I would do if everything were normal."

"Oh, Tina," Isla shook her head, moved deeply by the girl's words, "I hope Kyle won't be too angry –"

"With me? Pooh! I don't care. If he says anything, I will tell him."

"Should I leave a letter – to explain that it isn't your fault, or Costas? That I persuaded you –"

"No! I am not frightened of him." But the girl's face was suddenly wistful, as if at something lost, and Isla knew that things would never be the same again for her, with Kyle.

She ate what she could, drank her coffee, and then they set off to walk as far as the lake. This was not too far, and had the advantage of being well away from the house, a belt of trees separating it as well, so that they could not possibly be seen by anyone at the hotel.

It was glorious after the storm, trees newly washed, the leaves glossy and dark green, the flowers bursting with bright colours, the sky cloudless again, as if the storm had never been. But it had, and Isla would not forget. . . .

"Where is Kyle?" It hurt to say the name. "He'd gone

169

before you came."

"I know. He was up at the house early. I wondered why."

And I could probably tell you, thought Isla. But I won't. "Perhaps he couldn't sleep either," she said. A plane droned overhead and they looked up to see it, a silver bird whose wings glinted in the sun. A hope of escape, a way of leaving Kyle. . . . And soon she would be on one just like it, speeding away, perhaps flying over the hotel and looking out of the window to wave to Tina. . . . Isla shook her head irritably. She didn't know what was the matter with her. She was restless, longing to be away – and yet at the same time with a sense of utter desolation suddenly welling up inside her.

She began to walk more quickly, as if to shake the thoughts away, Tina skipped to catch up with her, laughing. "Oh, Isla, you are too fast for me! "

They stopped by the lake and sat upon the bench at its bank. Birds skimmed over the water, leaving faint ripples, reminding Isla of that other island and its swimming pool . . . Kyle's Kingdom. She supposed that he would set about claiming it legally, if he could. And there was his plane still there. How would they get that off? It didn't matter to her, of course. She had no doubt that he would organize its collection with the same efficiency he showed in everything else he did. Kyle . . . Kyle. . . . Why couldn't she stop thinking about him?

In desperation she turned to the girl who sat beside her.

"Will I see Cóstas today?" she asked.

"Of course. He will come after lunch to make sure that

all our plans are understood. He is enjoying helping you, Isla, truly."

"I can't tell you how grateful I feel. I'll never be able to repay all you've done for me."

Tina shook her head. "That's what friends are for." And she smiled.

When Costas came, at nearly five o'clock, he brought a bottle of wine with him. Isla had slept on the bed for an hour, and was feeling much better than she had before. She went to the door to greet him. "Hello, Costas. How nice to see you."

"Hello," his eyes were soft and dark upon her. "I thought we would have a drink." He looked at his sister. "Hey, go and bring in the glasses, little one."

She put her tongue out at him and ran out into the kitchen as he grinned and raised his hand as if to smack her. At least Tina would have Costas to defend her if Kyle became unpleasant, Isla thought, and that was a relief.

They drank the wine, and it went straight to Isla's head, leaving her pleasantly muzzy as evening drew on. The case was packed and locked and waiting in the bedroom. All she had to do in the morning was to leave.

Costas left at eight, not wanting to be there when Kyle arrived. Everything had to appear quite normal so that he would not suspect. As he stood in the doorway he touched Isla's arm lightly. "I will see you in the morning," he told her. "Sleep well."

"After that wine I will," she smiled. "Goodnight, Costas, and thank you for everything you're doing."

"The pleasure is mine. For you – anything." The last three words were spoken in a whisper, presumably so that Tina wouldn't hear. He took Isla's hand and lifted it to his mouth. "Goodnight, Isla," he said softly, and kissed her hand. She went back into the room pink-cheeked and saw Tina's grin. If she knew Tina, there would be some teasing after she had gone. After she had gone. . . .

She sat down, and Tina brought out the chess set. They began to play, and to wait for Kyle's arrival. The time was ticking slowly past, each minute taking her nearer to morning, and escape. The chessboard blurred, the chessmen seemed to take on a life of their own, almost to be dancing. Isla knew that not only was she tired but she wasn't entirely sober. Perhaps she would sleep well. She hoped so – the night – the *last* night there would be unbearable if she were to be lying awake for hours on end, with Kyle in the next room, a restless tiger, a man who had kissed her in a way no man had before, ever. And for what reason she thought she would never know.

CHAPTER ELEVEN

AND then it was morning. Isla had slept badly towards the end of the night, after a few hours of deep dreamless slumber, due no doubt to the wine she had drunk.

She woke before the dawn, and waited for it to come, and she didn't understand why she felt as she did. Surely she should be full of delight at the prospect of leaving – alone – for Rio? There was nothing inside her save a strange emptiness, a sensation of blankness, almost frightening.

The bedside clock ticked busily away, and that was the only sound. Silence from the living room. So Kyle still slept, unaware of what was so soon to happen; that his vigil would be over within a few hours.

She thought back to his arrival the previous night. He had been in a mood she had not encountered before, withdrawn, almost like a stranger. It had been quite late too, later that usual, so that Tina said, when he arrived:

"I must go now. My father will be wondering –" and she too had looked at him, then at Isla, as if puzzled. He had appeared not to notice, merely said, as he usually did:

"Come, I'll take you."

It was Isla's opportunity. As they went out of the door, after saying goodnight, she had gone into her bedroom and bolted her door. She could not face him, she knew. A few minutes later, when she had been under the shower in the bathroom, it seemed as if she had heard a knock at the bedroom door, a voice calling: "Isla? She had waited, ignoring it, pretending it was her imagination, and maybe it had been, for the sound had not been repeated.

She sat up in bed, about to switch on the light and look at a magazine when a faint crackling of twigs came from outside and she froze with her hand on the switch. Not again – not another intruder now. Quickly she ran to the window, leaving the room in darkness, and waited, heart beating fast, ready to shout for Kyle. . . .

But it wasn't necessary. She saw the man walk past – then drew in her breath sharply, almost on the point of a scream – and recognised him.

Kyle himself, returning to the chalet. Her heart still bumped with the first shreds of fear, but the beat was slowing, gradually becoming more normal as she accepted the fact that at least it was no intruder. No wonder there had been no sound from the living room. There had been no one there.

She heard the outer door open and then close quietly, and faint noises from the kitchen. But there would be no calling her this time. There was no storm. Isla dared not switch on the light now, lest he see it under the door. She went back and lay on the bed, waiting for the sudden burst of red-gold light which would announce the dawn.

One minute darkness; the next it was day. Her last day on Trintero. Isla crept out of bed and went to the bathroom to wash.

She heard Tina arrive, heard the voices as they spoke, as she put on lipstick seated at the dressing table. She brushed her hair, then slipped the brush into her make-up bag and zipped it up.

Unfastening her case, she put the cosmetic bag inside and laid her handbag on top. Everything was ready now for departure. She looked round to check that she had forgotten nothing. She dared not strip the bed in case Kyle looked in and saw, and became suspicious. There must be nothing, absolutely nothing amiss. Tina had already assured her that she would do all that was necessary after Isla's departure. She would have time, there on her own, until Isla was safely away, and she could emerge.

"Isla? It is me – Tina. Kyle has gone." There was suppressed excitement in the girl's voice, and Isla ran to the door to open it.

"Come in. I'm all ready. How long until Costas comes?"

"I don't know. He will be here for the case as soon as he can. You must eat your breakfast now."

"Yes, I will." They went into the kitchen, and Isla sat at the table and began to eat.

"I do not know what is the matter with Kyle." Tina's voice, as she said it, made Isla look up sharply.

"What do you mean?"

"He was – oh, I don't know," Tina shrugged prettily. "There was something about him – almost as if he were ill."

"Ill?" Isla said it more sharply than she intended and caught the girl's astonishment. "Ill?" she repeated more casually. "In what way?"

"I don't know. He looked as if he perhaps had not slept well –"

And that fact Isla already knew. She had seen him. But why should she care? She didn't, not at all. She shrugged.

"Oh well, perhaps it's his conscience. If he has one."

She looked at the clock on the wall. How the time was dragging! Only half a minute since she had last looked, and how many more to go?

She sipped at her orange juice. Tina lit the stove to make coffee. She was wearing the amethyst bracelet that Isla had given her, and it was obvious, from the way that she constantly moved her wrist about, as if to see the jewellery from a different angle, that she was delighted with the gift. Isla smiled to herself. She was pleased that she had thought of it. How much it could mean to Tina – and how little to herself. And she hadn't even missed her watch.

She could not eat much, but she was glad of the coffee, for it was hot and strong, and made her feel wide awake – and she felt as if she would need her wits about her for what lay ahead. She looked again at the clock. Surely it had stopped?

"Come, Isla, you must eat more than that. You are going a long way."

"I'm not hungry. I'll – I'll get something at Trintero Airport if I need to – don't worry about me, Tina, really."

"Oh, I wish I could go with you! It will be terrible here on my own."

"Why can't you? No one will miss you for a while."

"No." Tina shook her head. "If Kyle comes down Costas says I must tell him you are resting."

Costas had thought of everything! An unwilling smile

176

curved Isla's mouth. She didn't really feel like smiling.

When the tap came at the door, she jumped and looked quickly at Tina. Then Costas walked in. "Hello, I have come for the case. Kyle is having his breakfast. No, don't get up. I will get it – it is in the bedroom?"

"Yes. Thank you, Costas." Her mouth was dry. She watched him leave with it, and it somehow set the seal on what she was going to do. Soon he would return – and then –

She stood up and left the table, and went to the radio to switch it on. Anything so as not to have to think. Music filled the room, calypso music with an exciting beat, something she normally enjoyed, but not now.

Isla went to the window and looked out. Everything was beautiful and calm, the colours so bright, flowers and shrubs growing in splendid profusion outside, and the sun gilding everything so that the eyes almost hurt with the richness of it all. Isla put her hand to her eyes. They hurt, but it was not with the light. They ached with the effort it cost her not to cry.

And the door opened. Costas walked in.

"It is all ready, Isla. Shall we go now?" he asked.

"Yes. I'll get my handbag." Tina came out of the kitchen, wiping her hands on a towel. Isla turned to her to say goodbye, and the words died in her throat as she saw a look of utter horror come to the girl's face. "What –" she began, and a prickle ran down her spine as from behind her she heard Costas say:

"Kyle!" Isla turned slowly. Kyle was standing in the doorway, huge, tense, standing very still, not speaking – just looking at them all.

Then he broke the silence. "So I was right." He didn't seem angry, and strangely enough, Isla found that almost frightening.

She swallowed hard. Costas, she could see, had gone tense as well; he stood there watching Kyle, and Isla felt almost as if she were able to read his thoughts. He was ready for trouble. That was the last thing Isla wanted. "What do you mean – you were right?" she asked him, even though she knew the answer already.

"You're planning to leave. I guessed a day or so ago – and I've been watching, and having a word here and there – with Paul, for instance," and his glance flickered briefly to Tina as he said that. Tina came forward, her cheeks pink, dark eyes flashing as she answered:

"Then it is a pity you did not come here half an hour later, and Isla would have been safe from *you*!" Isla had never seen the girl in a temper before. She was young, and she had a spirit that could only be admired. "Why don't you go away from here – we don't want you!"

"Tina, don't –" Isla went to her and touched her arm. "Please, Tina. Don't upset yourself for me."

"It's all right, Isla – I'm not afraid of *him*!"

Then Costas spoke. "Tina – wait." He turned to Kyle. "You will not stop us. I will not let you." Brother and sister looked very much alike at that moment. There was a hardness to Costas' face she had never seen. His eyes too were darker with suppressed anger.

"No." Kyle spoke almost gently for him. "There will be no fight, Costas. I want to speak to Isla alone."

Isla went cold. She shook her head wordlessly, and Costas, seeing it, said:

"She does not wish to talk to you."

"She must." Kyle looked at Isla across the room. "Please, Isla."

Tension filled the air; it threatened to suffocate her. She was afraid – she knew not why, for what could Kyle do to hurt her further? Then Isla saw Costas step forward, saw his fists bunch, his stance, the readiness to tackle Kyle physically, and she knew there must be nothing to hurt these people who had helped her so much already.

"All right." She turned to Costas. "I'll speak to him."

"No, Isla. Just go now."

"I swear I only want to talk to Isla, that's all. It will take only a few minutes. Then you can go." He looked directly at Costas. "I'm not going to hurt her – even to touch her." Costas looked doubtfully at Isla, and she nodded.

"Please, Costas. I'll be all right. Please go outside." The fear had gone. Only an empty sensation remained.

"Very well. Come, Tina." He put out his arm. "We will be on the bench outside – if you want me, shout."

The two of them went out. Kyle closed the door.

"You can stay where you are to talk," Isla said. "You heard Costas. If you move any nearer to me I'll shout for him, I mean it, and it won't only be one man you'll have to fight, it'll be three of us."

Kyle nodded. Isla knew now what Tina had meant. He looked ill, haggard and drawn. "Don't worry," he said, and the merest flicker of a smile touched his mouth. "I don't fancy tackling Tina." But his eyes had a suddenly bleak look, and with a tiny stab of realization, Isla knew

179

that the girl's words had gone home with him.

She tilted her chin up. "I thought you wanted to talk," she said.

"Yes. I want to tell you why I tried to take you back to your father —"

"I already know," she cut in.

"No, you don't. Not the truth. Nobody knows that except your father and me — and now you're going to hear it, and when you've heard it, you can go." He patted his pockets and took out a packet of cigarettes and a lighter. "Do you want one?"

"No." She was waiting.

He lit a cigarette. "I've got a younger brother — a stepbrother, that is. We share the same mother. His name is Adam Ryder —" An elusive memory stirred in Isla's brain. Somewhere she had heard that name before. "Three years ago he went to work in one of your father's organizations in London. He has charm and good looks, and soon worked his way up to a position of trust." He moved and Isla instinctively backed slightly, but he was only reaching out to pick up an ashtray from a small table. "Unfortunately he abused that trust. I'll put it bluntly because I don't know any other way. He stole several thousands of pounds during those three years, and three months ago was found out by one of your father's accountants. That was when I got to hear of it — before the police were called in — and I went to see your father — to beg him to allow me to repay the money —" he stopped at Isla's expression of disgust.

Kyle gave her a twisted smile. "Yes, I know what you're thinking. Why should he steal, with such a wealthy brother – and why should he get away with it? I agree, he shouldn't. There's just one thing – no, two things – that made me go to your father as I did. The first, and most important is my – our mother. Adam is the apple of her eye – to her, he's perfect. He can do no wrong. All right, so she would find out he was just a fallible human after all – the only snag to that is the shock would literally kill her. She has a weak heart, has had for years, and is at present in a nursing home after another heart attack. I love my mother, Isla. I don't want her to die when she hears her son is a thief. I was prepared to do anything to keep that knowledge from her. My father left me a lot of money when he died. This sum to me was to be increased if my mother remarried – which she did. Adam is the son of that second marriage. Quite simply he resents my money, which he feels should have come to him through our mother. So he lived it up – fast cars, drinks, gambling – the lot – and managed to give everyone the impression that he was as wealthy as I am. The money had to come from somewhere – he stole it.

"Your father knew of me – and of my father. In a way they'd been business rivals, which must have made it all the sweeter for him to see John Quentin's son humbling himself, begging for mercy." He lifted his head. Just for a second Isla saw a trace of arrogant pride. "I've never done that before. I didn't like doing it then. But I did it because I had to. And I failed. Nobody steals from your father and gets away with it. He gave me a choice – to see Adam prosecuted – or to find you and bring you back." He stubbed out the half-smoked cigarette, grinding it almost to shreds. "I agreed to do it. He gave me a photo,

and two of your letters. That was all I had to go on, but
did it. I found you."

Isla had to sit down. She felt ill. "Go on," she said
dully.

"That's all. Except for one last thing. I didn't allow for
one certain basic fact of life." He stopped, and Isla looked
up at him. What did he mean? She wasn't prepared for
what she saw on his face. The look of agony in his eyes.

"I didn't – I wasn't prepared for what happened to
me." Their eyes met across the small space between
them. He went on, and his voice was harsher, deeper.
"God help me – I fell in love with you."

She didn't believe it. After what he had told her – it
was too pat, much too pat – and very cruel. But she
wouldn't let him see how deep the hurt went.

"You liar!" she breathed. "How can you – how dare
you?"

"No, I'm not lying. It's the truth – oh, I know you
wouldn't believe me – but I had to tell you. The time for
lies was over a few minutes ago, when I knew you were
going." He opened the door. "That's all. I didn't want
you to go back to Rio thinking what you did about me.
Don't worry, I shan't attempt to stop you, or follow you.
That much I owe you."

But surely he had told her this story to make her go
back? She didn't understand anything any more. Isla
stood up slowly. "So what do you do now? You told me it
would kill your mother –"

"I can't use you any more. Not now. I'm going back to
England to tell your father exactly what's happened, and
why I can't bring you back. And I never told him *where* I
182

found you, so you're safe. As for my mother, I'm going to do my damnedest to make sure she never finds out – I'll bribe the entire nursing home staff if necessary. And as for Adam, I'll think of something – better for her to think he's gone to Australia or something – I can fix letters up –"

"No," Isla said.

"No what?"

"Someone, somewhere, will let something slip. I can't – I can't have that on my conscience. I'll come back to Engand and face my father –"

"No." It was his turn to say it. "I'm not going to let you. You've been through hell with me, I'm only too well aware of that. If it's any consolation, I don't much like myself either."

"I thought I didn't. Until yesterday," said Isla.

"I'm sorry? Thought you didn't what?"

"Like you."

"I don't follow you." Yet something lit his eyes fleetingly – just for a second.

"I discovered – that the thought of leaving this place filled me with a great sadness. I thought it was because of Tina and Costas – and then, this morning, I realized it wasn't." She bit her lip.

"Then what was it?" But there was a tremor in his voice as he asked it.

"It was you. I knew I'd never see you again, that's all." And she looked at him.

He shook his head. "No. Oh, Isla, no. Not me."

"Yes, you." She walked forward slowly to him. "Do you want me to spell it out for you, Kyle?"

He reached out and gently, very gently, stroked her cheek. "Why me?"

"I don't know. Why anybody? But it's true – and I don't really want to go back to Rio any more, not if you're not there." She lifted her face up to him, and it was in her eyes now. The love shone out for him to see. He caught his breath.

"Isla," he whispered. "Isla. I can't – I can't –"

"Yes, you can. Kiss me, and then tell me you don't know."

He took her gently in his arms and kissed her, and when it was over he said, very quietly: "I believe you now, Isla, my love, my dearest one – what have I done to deserve you?"

She laughed softly. "I don't know. I'll think about it. Hadn't we better let Costas and Tina know – before they come charging in?"

He nuzzled her ears gently, and groaned. "Oh, God, I suppose so. Do you think she hates me?"

"She won't when I tell her the truth. They've both been wonderful, truly. Kyle, I will come back to England with you, you know. I don't mind – if you're there."

"Try and get rid of me! I may have knuckled under to your father once, but I won't do it again – ever." He smiled. "Can you believe that?"

"Oh yes, I can believe that."

There was a sharp knock at the door. Costas' voice. "Isla?"

"Come in."

He came in, followed by Tina. And they both stopped as they saw Isla and Kyle locked in each other's arms. It was Tina who recovered first, who managed to speak. "Isla – what is happening? Are you *safe*?"

"Safe?" What an appropriate word to use. A very appropriate word. "Oh yes, I'm quite safe," Isla agreed, and looked at Kyle. "You'd better sit down, both of you. We've got a lot to tell you – haven't we, Kyle?"

"A lot," he agreed gravely. "Quite a lot." And his arms were very strong and tender about Isla. They always would be.

THE OMNIBUS
Has Arrived!

A GREAT NEW IDEA
From HARLEQUIN

OMNIBUS — The 3 in 1 HARLEQUIN
only $1.50 per volume

Here is a great new exciting idea from Harlequin. THREE GREAT ROMANCES — complete and unabridged — BY THE SAME AUTHOR — in one deluxe paperback volume — for the unbelievably low price of only $1.50 per volume.

We have chosen some of the finest works of four world-famous authors . . .

VIOLET WINSPEAR

ISOBEL CHACE

JOYCE DINGWELL

SUSAN BARRIE

. . . and reprinted them in the 3 in 1 Omnibus. Almost 600 pages of pure entertainment for just $1.50 each. A TRULY "JUMBO" READ!

These four Harlequin Omnibus volumes are now available. The following pages list the exciting novels by each author.

Climb aboard the Harlequin Omnibus now! The coupon below is provided for your convenience in ordering.

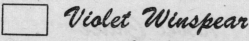

Violet Winspear
Omnibus

"To be able to reproduce the warmly exciting world of romance . . . a colourful means of escape", this was the ambition of the young VIOLET WINSPEAR, now a world famous author. Here, we offer three moving stories in which she has well and truly achieved this.

. . . . CONTAINING

PALACE OF THE PEACOCKS . . . where we join young Temple Lane, in the ridiculous predicament of masquerading as a youth on an old tub of a steamer, somewhere in the Java Seas. She had saved for five years to join her fiancee in this exotic world of blue skies and peacock waters — and now . . . she must escape him . . . (#1318).

BELOVED TYRANT . . . takes us to Monterey, where high mountainous country is alive with scents and bird-song above the dark blue surge of the Pacific Ocean. Here, we meet Lyn Gilmore, Governess at the Hacienda Rosa, where she falls victim to the tyranny of the ruthless, savagely handsome, Rick Corderas . . . (#1032).

COURT OF THE VEILS . . . is set in a lush plantation on the edge of the Sahara Desert, where Roslyn Brant faces great emotional conflict, for not only has she lost all recollection of her fiancee and her past, but the ruthless Duane Hunter refuses to believe that she ever was engaged to marry his handsome cousin . . . (#1267).

$1.50 per volume

Isobel Chace
Omnibus

A writer of romance is a weaver of dreams. This is true of ISOBEL CHACE, and her many thousands of ardent readers can attest to this. All of her eagerly anticipated works are so carefully spun, blending the mystery and the beauty of love.

. . . . CONTAINING

A HANDFUL OF SILVER . . . set in the exciting city of Rio de Janeiro, with its endless beaches and tall skyscraper hotels, and where a battle of wits is being waged between Madeleine Delahaye, Pilar Fernandez the lovely but jealous fiancee of her childhood friend, and her handsome, treacherous cousin — the strange Luis da Maestro . . . (#1306).

THE SAFFRON SKY . . . takes us to a tiny village skirting the exotic Bangkok, Siam, bathed constantly in glorious sunshine, where at night the sky changes to an enchanting saffron colour. The small nervous Myfanwy Jones realizes her most cherished dream, adventure and romance in a far off land. In Siam, two handsome men are determined to marry her — but, they both have the same mysterious reason . . . (#1250).

THE DAMASK ROSE . . . in Damascus, the original Garden of Eden, we are drenched in the heady atmosphere of exotic perfumes, when Vickie Tremaine flies from London to work for Perfumes of Damascus and meets Adam Templeton, fiancee of the young rebellious Miriam, and alas as the weeks pass, Vickie only becomes more attracted to this your Englishman with the steel-like personality . . . (#1334).

$1.50 per volume

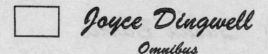

Joyce Dingwell
Omnibus

JOYCE DINGWELL'S lighthearted style of writing and her delightful characters are well loved by a great many readers all over the world. An author with the unusual combination of compassion and vitality which she generously shares with the reader, in all of her books.

. . . . CONTAINING

THE FEEL OF SILK . . . Faith Blake, a young Australian nurse becomes stranded in the Orient and is very kindly offered the position of nursing the young niece of the Marques Jacinto de Velira. But, as Faith and a young doctor become closer together, the Marques begins to take an unusual interest in Faith's private life . . . (#1342).

A TASTE FOR LOVE . . . here we join Gina Lake, at Bancroft Bequest, a remote children's home at Orange Hills, Australia, just as she is nearing the end of what has been a very long "engagement" to Tony Mallory, who seems in no hurry to marry. The new superintendent, Miles Fairland however, feels quite differently as Gina is about to discover . . . (#1229).

WILL YOU SURRENDER . . . at Galdang Academy for boys, "The College By The Sea", perched on the cliff edge of an Australian headland, young Gerry Prosset faces grave disappointment when her father is passed over and young Damien Manning becomes the new Headmaster. Here we learn of her bitter resentment toward this young man — and moreso. the woman who comes to visit him . . . (#1179).

$1.50 per volume

Susan Barrie

Omnibus

The charming, unmistakable works of SUSAN BARRIE, one of the top romance authors, have won her a reward of endless readers who take the greatest of pleasure from her inspiring stories, always told with the most enchanting locations.

. . . . CONTAINING

MARRY A STRANGER . . . Doctor Martin Guelder sought only a housekeeper and hostess for his home, Fountains Court, in the village of Herfordshire in the beautiful English countryside. Young Stacey Brent accepts his proposal, but soon finds herself falling deeply in love with him — and she cannot let him know . . . (#1043).

THE MARRIAGE WHEEL . . . at Farthing Hall, a delightful old home nestled in the quiet countryside of Gloucestershire, we meet Frederica Wells, chauffeur to Lady Allerdale. In need of more financial security, Frederica takes a second post, to work for Mr. Humphrey Lestrode, an exacting and shrewd businessman. Almost immediately — she regrets it . . . (#1311).

ROSE IN THE BUD . . . Venice, city of romantic palaces, glimmering lanterns and a thousand waterways. In the midst of all this beauty, Catherine Brown is in search of the truth about the mysterious disappearance of her step-sister. Her only clue is a portrait of the girl, which she finds in the studio of the irresistably attractive Edouard Moroc — could it be that he knows of her whereabouts? . . . (#1168).

$1.50 per volume

Each month from Harlequin

8 NEW FULL LENGTH ROMANCE NOVELS

Listed below are the latest three months' releases:

ALL BOOKS 60c

These titles are available at your local bookseller, or through the Harlequin Reader Service, M.P.O. Box 707, Niagara Falls, N.Y. 14302; Canadian address 649 Ontario St., Stratford, Ont.

T